Run Rabbit
Run

Other books by Barbara Michelhill

Storm Runners
Dangerous Diamonds

BARBARA MITCHELHILL

ANDERSEN PRESS
LONDON

First published in 2011 by
ANDERSEN PRESS LIMITED
20 Vauxhall Bridge Road, London SW1V 2SA
www.andersenpress.co.uk
Reprinted 2011

British Library Cataloguing in Publication Data available.

ISBN 978 1 84939 249 5

Printed and bound in Great Britain by CPI Bookmarque, Croydon CR0 4TD

*For Nia and Ivor whose Granny Joy told me
enough stories about her childhood in Wales
to fill a whole book — or two.*

A Knock at the Door

Waiting for a knock,
A knock at the door,
Hoping in silence
Please God no more.

Ellen Matthews, St Dominics Priory, Stone.

One

Rochdale, 1942

You know how it is when you've got a secret and you can't tell anybody? And you have to go to school and pretend everything's normal, even when you know it's not? Well, it was like that on the first day back after Christmas.

The war had been going on for ages – horrible things like rationing, blackouts and air-raid sirens happened all the time. On and on and on. But that day I had a secret, and I had something to look forward to.

'Heads down, children. Copy the sums into your exercise books,' said Miss Rossendale, who was teaching us now because Mr Taylor had joined the army to fight the Germans. I liked Mr Taylor. He was young with a big smiley face and he didn't shout like Miss Rossendale. She was very old, and she had wrinkles and wagged her finger a lot. But that day I didn't mind cos my secret was keeping me happy.

I didn't even mind when Podgy Watson, who sat next to me on the front row, whispered nasty things about my dad. And I wasn't bothered at break when nobody would play with me except Brenda Watkins, who suffered from rashes.

The secret was special. 'Not a word, mind,' Dad had said when he told me. 'Not even to our Freddie. We'll tell him soon enough. It'll be just the two of us for now.' Which had made me feel very grown-up.

That wasn't the only secret we shared. Two months ago, after the bomb fell on Mum's shop and killed her, Dad told me another one. 'Can you see that star, Lizzie?' he'd asked once when I couldn't sleep.

There were a lot of stars in the sky that night but he'd pointed his finger at the brightest, shiniest one of all.

'There's your mum,' he'd said, tapping his nose like he does when he tells me secrets. 'So now you know she'll always be there, twinkling away, watching out for us.'

It's true. I see her every night as clear as anything. Sometimes we chat. Except when it's cloudy.

But Dad's new secret was different, and all day at school I couldn't think about anything else. The first lesson of the afternoon was geography and Podgy Watson left me alone because he was concentrating on a scab on his knee. He said it looked like a map of Africa and he spent most of the lesson picking it off and eating it. But when he'd finished he looked across at me and smirked and I could tell that he'd come up with a new way to torment me. He reached for a red crayon and started to write; when he was finished he slid the piece of paper onto my desk.

I shouldn't have read it. I knew it would be bad. But I couldn't help it.

EVERYBODY KNOWS YOUR DAD KILLED YOUR MUM
THAT'S WHY THEY WON'T HAVE HIM
IN THE ARMY

I could feel my face flush red and I screwed the paper into a ball. It was a horrible thing to say. Terrible! *A lie!*

So I jabbed him in the leg with my compass.

Twice.

It wasn't much. No more than a pinprick, really. But he screamed like a stuck pig, 'Aaaaahhhhgggg!' and jumped out of his seat, holding onto his leg and waving his arm in the air. 'Miss! Miss!' he called out. 'Lizzie Butterworth stabbed me! Miss, I'm bleeding!'

Miss Rossendale, who was at the back of the classroom helping Brenda Watkins with her writing, looked over. Podgy was leaping up and down, squealing and yelling and clutching onto his leg as Miss Rossendale marched to the front with a face as black as thunder.

Now I was for it. I pushed my glasses further onto my nose, sat up straight and looked innocent. I held my breath and waited for the teacher to speak.

She stood in front of our desk, leaned forward and frowned – which made the wrinkly lines between her eyes even deeper so she looked like Dracula. Really! My heart was beating at a hundred miles an hour as she raised her hand and pointed her finger. But she wasn't pointing it at me.

'Roger Watson!' she shouted. 'This is the behaviour of a three-year-old not an eleven-year-old boy. Mr Taylor has left me instructions on how to deal with you. Now go to Miss Oxley's room and she will give you the punishment you deserve.'

What an escape! She hadn't even checked Podgy's leg for damage. Mr Taylor would have done.

'It was her, miss,' he protested. 'I didn't do nothing!'

But Miss Rossendale stretched out her arm and pointed at the door. 'Go!' she said, and he limped out of the classroom, his head bowed. We didn't see him for the rest of the day.

When the bell went for home time, I walked towards the gate as usual, but immediately saw Podgy standing on the corner of Derby Street with four of his mates. Just in case they were waiting for me, I hung back for ten minutes, hoping they would go. When they didn't, I decided to walk out, bold as you like, as if I hadn't seen them.

'Hey!' called Podgy. 'I want to speak to you, Lizzie Butterworth.'

I knew I was in trouble. I pretended not to hear. I stuffed my hands in my coat pockets and kept walking.

But Podgy and his gang crossed over and headed towards me. 'Got wax in your ears, have yer?' he said, barging me with his shoulder so that I came to a halt. His mates made a circle around me. I couldn't escape. Five against one.

'I've heard things about your dad, I have,' Podgy said with a sneer. 'Everybody's talking. Why hasn't he joined up, eh? Doesn't he know there's a war on?'

'Course he does,' I said.

'Then why isn't he off fighting? *Our* dads are over in France, aren't they, lads?'

4

'Yeah, they are,' the gang agreed, sounding like a flock of *baaa*-ing sheep.

They moved forward and closed in on me. 'Go on,' said Podgy, 'why hasn't he joined up? Eh? Eh? Eh?'

I glanced about, hoping someone might come to my rescue, but the kids who were passing just pretended not to notice and hurried home.

Podgy lifted his fat fist and punched my shoulder so that I staggered back and slipped on the wet pavement, banging my head on the flagstones and sending my glasses and my gas-mask case flying.

'Go on, say it! He's a coward,' yelled Podgy as he grabbed my coat collar and heaved me into a standing position. 'Your dad's too scared to fight.'

'He's not scared!' I shouted as loud as I could. 'He's a conscientious objector.'

Nobody spoke. Then Podgy shoved me away, pinning me against the wall. 'And what's that in plain English?'

I tried to keep my voice calm even though I was shaking inside. 'A conscientious objector doesn't believe in killing people. They don't believe it's right to go to war.'

Podgy stepped back, folding his arms across his chest and smiling a nasty, mean sort of smile. 'I've heard my mum talk about men like your dad. They call 'em conchies. She says it's just another word for coward.' Then he moved forward and spat in my face.

The spittle dripped onto my coat while the gang whooped and clapped and called, 'Conchie Coward! Conchie Coward!

Conchie Coward!' while they jigged around in a circle like a pack of Red Indians on the warpath.

Podgy stood rocking with laughter and that's when I took my chance. I lowered my head and rammed it hard into his stomach. WAM!

His mouth fell open in surprise as the breath was forced out of him. His feet skidded on the pavement and he crashed into his mates, dragging them down with him until they were all lying in one great, wet heap.

I didn't hang around, of course. I grabbed my glasses and gas-mask case, and scarpered. If they caught me I'd be history. They were shouting after me but I kept running until I reached the end of the street and then I tore round the corner into Durham Road.

It was there that I ran slap bang into Aunt Dotty.

Two

Dad says family is very important. But I don't think Aunt Dotty can be *real* family. She's supposed to be Dad's sister, but she's not a bit like him. She's a mean, skinny old witch who never laughs. I think Granny must have found her on the doorstep in a basket when she was a baby – but no one's ever said. Being abandoned can't be very nice though. No wonder Aunt Dotty has a terrible temper.

'Speak when you're spoken to,' she often says. Or, 'Watch your manners or you'll get what for.' Or, 'There'll be no tea for you, my girl.'

Knowing what she was like, I wouldn't have bumped into her that day on purpose – but I didn't know she was round the corner with our Freddie, did I?

She made a terrible fuss, as if I'd done it on purpose. She squealed and cried, 'Oh, oh,' while she straightened her hat and brushed down her coat. Then she glared at me with her mean little eyes. 'Why can't you look where you're going, stupid child?'

My cousin, Toffee-nosed Pat, was with them and she loved to see me in trouble. 'Lizzie's been fighting,' she said, pointing to the cut on my chin. 'It's that school, Mother. There are some awful children there.' She looked at me and smirked. 'You should go to the convent school like me. We have a proper uniform and everything. It's ever so nice.'

Aunt Dotty, still in a temper, grabbed hold of my coat collar and marched me down the street. 'Home, my girl,' she snapped.

Every afternoon Aunt Dotty fetched Freddie from the infant school and took him to our house. I would join them and then she waited with us till Dad came back from work. But today, thanks to Podgy Watson, I was a few minutes late getting home and she'd come looking for me.

'Get those wet things off before you catch your death of cold,' she said when we got home. 'Just look at the state of you. What would your mother say if she knew you'd been fighting?'

I thought of Mum with her red curls and her big smile and I knew what she'd say: 'You're a bad 'un, sure enough, our Lizzie – just like me at your age.' And then she'd roar with laughter and wrap her arms around me in a big hug. That was Mum, and I couldn't help smiling at the thought of her.

Aunt Dotty must have seen. 'So you think it's funny, do you?' she cried, lashing out, grabbing hold of my ear and pulling me towards her with such a force that I cried in pain. 'I'll teach you to laugh at me.' She shook me like a rag doll before slapping me hard across my legs. 'Let that be a lesson.' She smacked me again so hard that my leg stung as if I'd been attacked by a dozen wasps. I gritted my teeth determined not to cry. I wouldn't! She didn't stop. She slapped me again. She wouldn't be satisfied until she'd made me.

It was only when our Freddie screamed, 'No! Don't you hurt my sister!' that she let her hand fall to her side and turned away.

Her face was screwed up with anger as she went over to the table and cut a loaf into slices, spreading them with dripping. When she was done, she pointed the knife at me and said, 'Not a word from you, my lady. Now sit down and eat your tea.'

There were three plates. She put bread and dripping on two of them. The other was empty until she fetched a brown paper parcel from her shopping basket, took out two strawberry-jam sandwiches and put them on Pat's plate.

'Thank you, Mother,' said Toffee-nosed Pat, picking up her sandwich and smirking at us. She did this every day, and every day we watched her bite into the jam and wished that we could taste it. But we never did.

The table was by the window overlooking the mill opposite. That day I sat there, feeling my leg stinging from the slaps and I looked up at the darkening sky and blinked my eyes dry.

Lucky the stars weren't out yet, I thought. If Mum had been looking down...well, she'd have gone barmy seeing Aunt Dotty hitting me like that.

I ate my sandwich slowly, hoping that Dad would come home before I'd finished it. He would cheer me up.

But when he did arrive, I was confused. I thought he'd rush in, all happy and glad to be home. But no. His shoulders drooped; his forehead was wrinkled with worry lines. Had he forgotten our secret? Wasn't it the most exciting secret in the world? I wondered.

He sat on the empty chair at the table while Aunt Dotty brewed a pot of tea. 'So what happened at the appeal?' she asked.

'What's an appeal?' Freddie wanted to know.

'It's when some important people ask you lots of questions,' Dad told him.

'What questions?'

'About why I don't want to fight in the war.'

Aunt Dotty looked at Dad and scowled. 'I suppose you gave them a lot of fancy words, did you?'

Dad looked up at her. 'I told them what I told that committee two months ago – I didn't believe in war and that I wouldn't go killing anybody. War is bad, that's what I said. There was no good to be gained from fighting wars.'

'And they let you off to go and plant potatoes, did they?'

Dad sighed and shook his head. 'I didn't stand a chance. Major Thompson and Doctor Hill were on the appeal committee.'

'Well, they wouldn't be impressed,' said Aunt Dotty, who couldn't stop a mean little smile spreading across her face. 'Both the major and the doctor fought in the first war, and their sons are out there fighting now. What did they say?'

'They told me I should join the army. "You're young enough and strong enough," they said. "None of this silly talk about not wanting to fight." They thought I was making excuses. They thought I was a coward.'

Aunt Dotty stood there with her arms folded. 'So they won't let you be a conchie?'

'The lady on the committee said they might let me work in the munitions factory. But I said no. I won't make bombs and bullets that will kill people.'

10

'Well, that's it then.'

'But why won't they let me carry on working at the yard? I do useful work. I keep those lorries running, don't I?' He ran his fingers through his hair and frowned. 'They said if I don't report to the barracks tomorrow, I'll be sent to prison.'

'Just what I thought. So you'll just have to join up like everybody else.'

'I will not!' Dad snapped. 'I'm not fighting in any war.'

She wagged her finger at him. 'They were right. You *are* a coward! Nothing but a coward!'

'No. Not that,' said Dad, and he pushed back his chair and stood facing her.

We all stared at them, thinking they were going to have a proper fight. Freddie started to cry, so Dad turned round and picked him up.

'My children have suffered already, Dotty. Wasn't the bombing bad enough – taking their mother like that? I'll make sure they don't lose me an' all. We stay together.'

'Oh and how can you stay together if you're in prison?' asked Aunt Dotty, her face flushing pink.

By then, Freddie was crying louder than ever and Dad hugged him tight, trying to quieten him. 'I've already made plans. We're going away.'

I couldn't believe it. Dad had told her our secret. He *promised* it was our secret. Now she'd tell everybody. That was what she was like.

She stood with her hands on her hips. 'I might have guessed you'd go on the run,' she sneered. 'And what'll happen when they find you? You'll finish up in prison anyway.'

The argument continued until Aunt Dotty said, 'I won't listen to another word,' and turned to fetch her coat. 'If you won't join up, there's no more to be said, is there? Ready, Patricia?'

As she opened the door to step onto the street, she turned and looked at Dad. 'If you can't behave like a man and fight, then you're no brother of mine and I'll not have anything to do with you ever again. Our mother would be ashamed of you.'

I jumped up from my chair, shaking with anger. 'Don't you speak to my dad like that!' I yelled. '*Your* mother would be ashamed of *you*!'

Aunt Dotty's mouth fell open and her face changed to a peculiar shade of purple. Without another word, she marched out with her head in the air, followed by Toffee-nosed Pat.

Freddie stopped crying as soon as they'd gone. Dad winked at me and sat Freddie on his knee. He was going to tell him our secret. That was all right. My brother had to know sometime.

'I've got something to tell you, little chap,' he said. 'Tomorrow morning, we'll get up very early.'

'Why?' asked Freddie.

'Because we're going on holiday.'

'Are we going to Blackpool?'

Dad shook his head. 'No. We're going to Gloucestershire,' he said. 'Would you like that?'

But Freddie didn't know where Gloucestershire was and he started crying again.

'It's in the country,' I said. 'There'll be cows and sheep and things.'

'We're going to a place called Whiteway,' Dad said, 'and we'll have a grand time.'

But there was one thing worrying me. I had to ask. 'Will the police come looking for us, Dad? Will they take you to prison like Aunt Dotty said?'

'No one will find us, Lizzie. It will be our secret place.' He gave me a hug and then he said, 'Mr Hollingsworth from the builders' yard is going to take us in his lorry. His brother lives at Whiteway and we're going to stay with him.'

At the mention of riding in a lorry, Freddie's eyes grew wide with excitement and he grinned. For him it was even better than going on holiday.

Of course, I knew we weren't going on holiday. Who goes on holiday in January? But Freddie was only six. He didn't know that.

'How long are we going for, Dad?' I asked.

Dad looked at me and shook his head. 'I don't know, Lizzie, that all depends on Mr Hitler.'

Three

Very early the next morning, Dad woke me up. 'Get dressed, Lizzie. Time to go.'

It was freezing so I got dressed under the bedclothes. With a bit of wriggling I pulled on my socks, my vest and knickers, my thickest jersey and my wool skirt, then I flung back the blankets and jumped out. On with shoes and glasses. Job done.

Dad had already carried Freddie downstairs.

I blew out the candle and opened the blackout curtains. The window was covered in frost but I rubbed a circle in it so I could look up into the still-dark sky, just to check that Mum was there. She was. Twinkling brightly, as usual. 'We're going away,' I said – but I think she already knew.

Freddie and I ate bread and cheese, washed our faces in the sink in the back kitchen and went to the lav in the yard.

Those were the last things we did in our house in Norwich Street.

'Coats,' Dad ordered, then we pulled on the balaclavas Granny had knitted last winter and Dad put his cap on before he opened the door. We all stepped out onto the street holding our gas masks and the suitcases we had packed the night before.

We walked with our heads down, the bitterly cold wind whipping round our legs.

Mr Hollingsworth was meeting us at the builders' yard at the top of our road. Dad had worked there ever since he left school. Sometimes, in the holidays, he'd take us and show us round – and we loved that. The yard was crammed with all sorts of things: stacks of bricks, piles of wood, bags of cement. And, to make it more exciting, there were plenty of rats running under the sheds and between bags of plaster. Sometimes Dad set traps and I watched him, worried that he'd catch his fingers – but he never did. Our dad was really clever. He mended the lorries when they broke down and he knew about building houses and that. No problem.

That morning, an open-back lorry was parked under the sign that read R & T HOWARTH BUILDERS MERCHANTS, and I saw Mr Hollingsworth leaning against the cab. We waved and he waved back. 'How do, Will?' he called. 'How do, Lizzie, Freddie?'

Freddie raced ahead. 'We're going on holiday,' he said, jumping up and down in front of Mr Hollingsworth.

'Are you indeed?' he laughed. 'Then we'd better get started.'

Dad lifted us into the cab. Mr Hollingsworth climbed in the other side and sat in the driver's seat so that all four of us were squashed up together.

'Everybody ready?' he asked, putting the key in the ignition.

'Ready!' we answered and we cheered when the engine started with a roar and we set off.

As we drove down Norwich Street, we passed our house – I'd lived there for eleven years, ever since I was born – and I thought about Mum. How she had played hopscotch with us on the flags outside our front door and helped us make dens in the back yard. I tried not to feel sad because I knew she was up there watching us. I bet she was waving.

When we reached the end of the street and pulled onto the main road, Dad said, 'Thanks for giving us a lift, Reg. It's very good of you.'

'Say nowt about it, lad,' Mr Hollingsworth answered, puffing at his old pipe. 'You'll be safe enough at Whiteway. And you nippers will have a grand old time. You'll have woods and fields to run about in and Arthur will see you right.'

'Is Arthur your brother?' I asked.

He nodded. 'He built a house in Whiteway years ago. In the middle of a wood. It's not big but you'll like it.'

'Is it like Red Riding Hood's house?' Freddie wanted to know.

'Not exactly. There aren't any wolves.'

There were lots of things I wanted to know about his brother too. After all, we were going to live with him and I knew Mr Hollingsworth wouldn't mind if I asked. 'Why did your brother go to Whiteway? Why didn't he stay in Rochdale, like you?'

Mr Hollingsworth waited at the traffic lights before turning right behind a double-decker bus. 'It's a long story,' he said. 'But I'll tell you, if you like' – he drew on his pipe and puffed out a stream of grey smoke before he continued – 'Arthur was only eighteen when the first war started against Germany. He went and joined up because he thought it would be a great adventure. He wanted to travel to countries he'd never seen.'

'And did he?'

16

'He went to a place in Belgium called Ypres – the English soldiers called it Wipers.'

'Did he have an adventure in Wipers?' Freddie asked.

'No. He was stuck in dirty trenches in the freezing cold with no lavatories and bullets flying around.'

'That's not an adventure,' said Freddie. 'I would have come home straight away.'

'Well, he couldn't. He had to stay and fight the Germans.'

Freddie looked up at Dad. 'Why don't *you* fight the Germans? They dropped that bomb on Mum, didn't they?' he said. 'That's only fair.'

Dad shook his head. 'But that would make me just like the people who killed her, wouldn't it?' he said. 'If we all refused to fight there wouldn't be a war at all.'

After that Dad went quiet for a bit and looked out of the side window. I suppose he was thinking about Mum, but I wanted to hear more about Mr Hollingsworth's brother.

'What happened in Wipers?'

'The Germans had a terrible weapon called mustard gas. Arthur said it was horrible greeny-yellow stuff that drifted across the battlefields towards the soldiers.'

'Like smoke?'

He nodded. 'Aye, and they breathed it in. Thousands of soldiers died. Most of Arthur's friends did.' Mr Hollingsworth sighed and drew on his pipe again. 'After that our Arthur hated war with a vengeance. "What's the point of it all?" he used to say.'

'But he didn't die, did he?'

'No. But the gas injured his lungs so much that he could hardly breathe.' Mr Hollingsworth looked sad. 'He was sent back to England and stayed in hospital for a long time. While he was there a man in the next bed told him about Whiteway. He said that some people had set up a commune, living and working together, with their own rules. They didn't believe in war and they welcomed anyone.'

'Anyone?'

'Anyone who was in trouble. People escaping their own country. People who didn't want to fight – they were called conscientious objectors.'

'Like our dad,' I said.

'Like your dad.'

'So your brother decided to go to Whiteway?'

'Aye. He thought it sounded just the place for him so he went, and he's lived there ever since.'

All this time, Dad had sat staring out not saying a word. Mr Hollingsworth must have noticed because he said, 'Don't worry, Will. You're doing the right thing. Remember all those lads killed in the first war? Young lives cut short. Wives and mothers grieving. And for what? The Germans are back again. How many more will die before it's over?'

Dad didn't answer.

'Just think about it, Will. You've already lost your wife. Killing Germans won't bring her back, will it?' He pulled his pipe from his mouth and wagged it at Dad. 'You keep out of this rotten war. Mark my words, lad. There's nowt good going to come of it.'

We all sat there in a terrible sad silence until Freddie, who didn't like silence at all, started to sing:

> *'Run, rabbit, run, rabbit, run, run, run.*
> *Run, rabbit, run, rabbit, run, run, run.*
> *Bang, bang, bang, bang goes the farmer's gun.*
> *Run, rabbit, run, rabbit, run, run, run.*
> *Run, rabbit, run, rabbit, run, run, run.*
> *Don't give the farmer his fun, fun, fun.*
> *He'll get by without his rabbit pie,*
> *So run, rabbit, run, rabbit, run, run, run.'*

And we all joined in.

Funny that he should choose that song because we were on the run just like the rabbit.

Four

Mr Hollingsworth dropped us in Birmingham, where a man with a van was waiting to take us on to Whiteway.

'Mr Butterworth?' he called out before we'd reached him.

'Yes, that's me,' Dad shouted. 'We're coming.'

The man was as wide as he was tall and his head was the shape of a football, resting on his shoulders without any sign of a neck. He had black button eyes which almost disappeared into red puffy cheeks. His overcoat didn't fasten across his bulging stomach and I saw that he was wearing a striped apron underneath.

I thought he might introduce himself or say 'Hello' or be a bit friendly. But no. 'I've got a delivery to make in Stroud,' he said. 'The girl will have to go in the back.'

Dad looked at me. 'Will you be all right, Lizzie?'

'She'll have to be,' snapped the man with the van.

'I'll be all right,' I said. 'I can sit on the suitcases.'

The van was black with white lettering edged in gold that read, HOBBS AND SONS, FINE BUTCHERS SINCE 1904.

While Dad got into the front with Freddie, the man opened the doors at the back for me to climb in.

'Don't mess around with anything,' he growled.

I lifted the suitcases and pushed them inside, but straight away I smelled the most disgusting, sickening smell. I clamped my hand over my mouth and nose, trying to block it out. Then I noticed a bundle on the floor of the van, something was wrapped up in a sheet and there was a foot sticking out at the end nearest me.

Now I knew what the smell was. It was a dead sheep.

'I can't go in there, mister. Honest,' I said, screwing up my face. 'I can't stand the smell. I'll be sick.'

The man frowned. 'Get in, girl,' he snapped, raising his hand and pushing me inside before he slammed the doors shut.

I thought of calling out to Dad but I didn't want to make a fuss or we might have to walk to Whiteway, and we didn't have a map.

I sat on the suitcases, pinching my nose to block out the smell with one hand, and holding onto a bar on the side of the van with the other. As we moved away I managed to steady myself, but the sheep kept sliding about and banging against my legs every time we went round a bend. Worse, the smell got stronger because there were no windows to open. With no fresh air to let it escape the smell got so bad that my head began to throb, my eyes hurt and everything started to spin. Then my belly joined in with a grumbling ache. The more we bumped along, the sharper the pain.

It got so bad that the contents of my stomach began to gurgle and finally they shot up into my throat. I tried to hold in the sick by pressing my lips together and clamping my hand over my mouth, but I knew I couldn't hold it for much longer.

I banged on the thin partition between the cab and me. 'Dad!' I called out.

Big mistake.

As I spoke, the vomit erupted, spraying the walls, the floor and, worst of all, the dead sheep.

The man in the apron must have heard the commotion. He slammed on the brakes, which sent me flying to the back of the van. Then he came running round and flung the doors open. 'What the...?' he gasped as he looked inside.

I couldn't speak. I was bent double clutching my stomach and groaning.

'Ruined!' he shouted, and he dragged me out and dumped me on the side of the road followed by the suitcases and our gas masks. 'Just look at my meat. How can I sell it now?'

By then Dad and Freddie had joined me. Dad rubbed my aching stomach, while Apron Man dragged the sheet off the carcass.

'Ruined!' he repeated as he crawled inside the van. He used a cloth to wipe up my sick as best he could and when most of it was cleared, he pulled off his apron and wrapped it around the carcass.

'Kids,' he growled. 'More trouble than they're worth. I should never have agreed...'

Dad tried to apologise, but Apron Man wouldn't listen. 'You're all alike, you conchies. You make trouble for other people. You want something for nothing.'

'You'll get paid just as we agreed,' Dad said. 'But we didn't agree to travel with a dead sheep. No wonder my daughter was sick.'

'I'm delivering that mutton to a customer, ain't I? I can't get the petrol just to run folks like you about. I've got to earn a living.'

I knew meat was rationed; sometimes you couldn't get any at all – except if you had a pile of money. 'Our teacher told us about people who sell meat on the black market,' I said. 'Don't you know you'll go to jail if you get found out?'

He glowered at me. 'So who's going to tell, eh? Not you for a start, lady. Your dad's more likely to go to jail than me' – he paused as if he was wondering what to do – 'I've had enough of you. You can walk the rest of the way.'

Dad was furious, of course, and he grabbed the man by his shirt collar. 'You leave us here and you won't get paid. Not only that, I'll drop a note into the nearest police station letting them know…'

'All right. All right,' said the man, holding up his hands. 'Get back in then – just as long as she ain't sick again.'

We somehow crammed into the front of the van, and for the rest of the journey, no one spoke. The man just gritted his teeth and stared at the road ahead as the rain fell and the windscreen wipers squeaked.

I didn't care. It wouldn't be long before we reached Whiteway.

Five

You know when you think you're nearly there and the driver stops and tells you you'll have to walk the last bit, then your dad gets mad and they argue about money? Well, it was like that.

Dad handed over some coins.

'Not enough,' said the man.

'That will have to do,' Dad insisted.

More arguing.

As we started to walk away the man shouted, 'I hope the police get you, you coward! You're a disgrace to your country, you are.' Then he climbed back into his van and roared off in a terrible rage.

How rude was that? He really should control his nasty temper.

Freddie wanted to know if we were at the seaside.

'No, son. We're in the country, remember?' Dad lifted him up so that he could see over the hedge. 'Look, there are cows in that field.'

The rain had almost stopped but there was an icy wind, so we pulled on our balaclavas again and wrapped our scarves tight around our necks before we set off.

We'd been going for about ten minutes when an open-back lorry came along the road and pulled up not far away. A man with a fine moustache wound down the window and leaned

24

out. 'Do you chaps want a lift?' he called.

Dad hurried over to talk to him. 'That would be grand,' he said. 'Are you going anywhere near Whiteway?'

The man with the moustache laughed. 'Well, there's a thing. I'm actually going up to Whiteway. Where are you staying?'

Dad grinned. 'With Arthur Hollingsworth. Do you know him?'

'Arthur! Ah, yes. Good old chap, eh?' Then he opened the door and jumped out of the cab. 'I'm Basil, by the way.'

'Pleased to meet you,' said Dad, shaking his hand. 'I'm Will, and this is Lizzie and Freddie.'

Basil bowed as if we were royalty. 'Delighted to make your acquaintance, ma lady, young sir.' We giggled and I did a curtsey and almost fell over. The man threw his head back and roared with laughter so that his moustache wobbled, which made us laugh even more.

'Come on,' he said as he helped us onto the back of the lorry. 'Find a nice space between the sacks of flour and hold onto the sides. It won't take long. Think of it as a ride at the fairground – a bit bumpy, don't you know?'

He was right about the bumpy ride, but it was still miles better than being in that van with the dead sheep. Once we'd turned off the road and started up the lane to Whiteway, it was just bare earth and stones and plenty of potholes. We were tossed around like sacks of carrots, but suddenly Basil stopped the lorry and jumped down.

'Come and take a look at Whiteway. You can get a good view from here,' he said, pointing into the distance. 'Some of the houses are hidden among the trees but look over there. See? That's Mrs Weaver's house.'

I was surprised to see what looked like a garden shed. 'Does she live there?'

'Oh yes. And here's a funny thing...'

'What?'

'She's a weaver. Now how about that for a surprise?'

'I don't believe you,' said Freddie.

'Well, it's true, my man. She weaves blankets and all kinds of clothes. And she knits – jumpers, gloves, scarves, all sorts. And look – behind Mrs Weaver's is Professor Elstein's house.' This had a very pointy roof with a window in it, so he must have a bedroom upstairs. But it looked rather crooked and had a tall chimney that leaned to one side. 'The professor has been here for twenty years,' Basil continued. 'Very clever. Speaks several languages and writes books.' Then he pointed over to the right. 'And there,' he said, 'that's where I live.'

We could see fields and woods and twisting pathways but we couldn't see another house, just an old railway carriage.

'You don't live in that, do you?'

Basil grinned. 'Pretty special, eh? Come to tea when you're settled in and take a look around.'

I couldn't think of anywhere more exciting to live than in a railway carriage. 'Thanks, Basil. We'll come soon.'

We jumped back onto the lorry and drove on up the hill past two more cottages, which were no bigger than Mrs Weaver's. Then we went by one house, which was not quite finished.

'There's Edek Nowac and his family, they're from Poland,' said Basil, nodding at the building.

A man was sitting on the unfinished roof while his wife passed him a hammer and nails.

'Ahoy there!' Basil called as he pulled up. A boy and girl who were playing in the mud looked over and smiled. 'Need any help, Edek?' he asked their father.

The man raised his hand. 'Nearly finished, Basil. Thank you. But we need more wood, please.'

'Okey-doke,' said Basil, 'I'll see what I can do tomorrow, old chap.'

The family waved as we set off again and once we reached the top of the hill where the ground flattened out, Basil switched off the engine.

'This is it, ladies and gentlemen,' he called, opening the door and jumping down. 'Come on, I'll show you to Arthur's house.'

'Is Arthur nice?' asked Freddie as Basil lifted him off the lorry.

'Mr Hollingsworth to you,' said Dad, who was always telling us to watch our manners.

'Yes, young man,' said Basil. 'He's a good old cove. He'll give you a splendid welcome.'

He led us down a narrow, winding path, with bare-branched trees overhanging. I noticed he'd got a limp and he walked in a funny lopsided kind of way like Long John Silver. Freddie and I started copying him – loppity-loo, loppity-loo – till Dad grabbed us by the shoulders and told us to walk properly.

A little further on, Basil called over his shoulder, 'This is it!' and he pointed ahead where the path opened out.

I had dreamed of this moment all the way from Rochdale. I couldn't wait to see this house. I was expecting it to be made of bricks, with a roof and a chimney and a neat little garden. But Mr Hollingsworth's house was built from planks of wood with sheets of corrugated iron on the roof. There was a wooden door with a black latch and on either side were windows which didn't match at all. Some piles of logs were stacked nearby alongside a heap of scrap iron, bits of old machinery and a large water butt. It was a surprising, higgledy-piggledy kind of place.

We raced towards the front door, but before we got there it opened and a large collie came bounding out. Freddie was terrified and clung to me. I suppose a dog looks big when you're only five.

Then a voice boomed from the house. 'Jip! Here, boy! Here!' and a tall man – with a rounded belly and big white beard – stepped out. He looked so like our Mr Hollingsworth that we knew it had to be his brother, Arthur.

'And who have you found lurking in the woods, Basil?' he called over our heads.

'Dangerous criminals, I fear,' Basil replied.

Mr Hollingsworth leaned forward, squeezing his eyes as if he wanted to get a better look at us. But I saw the grin spread across his face.

'Ah, no, they're not criminals, Basil! They're Lizzie and Freddie! I've been expecting them.' He laughed at his joke before bending his knees and spreading his arms wide. Freddie raced up to him and was swept into the air and twirled around, squealing and laughing while Jip barked and pranced about on his hind legs.

When things calmed down, Mr Hollingsworth took my hand and kissed it as if I were a princess. 'Welcome to my humble abode, Miss Elizabeth,' he said, and then he shook Dad's hand and smiled and patted him on the shoulder. 'You'll be all right here, Will.'

It was a warm welcome.

'Come in, all of you,' he said. 'The kettle's boiling.'

'Thanks all the same, old boy,' said Basil. 'No time, I'm afraid. Got to get back to the bakery with the flour. Tomorrow's bread, don't you know?'

Dad turned and shook Basil's hand. 'Thank you for the lift. I'm very grateful.'

Basil smiled. 'Good luck, old chap. See you around, no doubt. Toodle-pip.' And he limped away down the path towards his lorry while we stepped inside the house and closed the door behind us.

Six

Mr Hollingsworth's house smelled of wood and was as warm as toast. There was a large black stove with a metal pipe rising up out through the roof and, most amazing of all, old carpets were hung on the walls to stop cold sneaking through the gaps in the wood. They were in every colour you could think of. Red, blue, yellow, brown...The patterns were faded but they were still beautiful. Over our head woollen blankets had been stretched across the rafters.

It was like being inside a big, cosy tent.

Mr Hollingsworth lifted a brown enamel teapot off a shelf. 'First things first,' he said. 'You make yourselves at home while I brew us a nice pot of tea.'

We hung our coats on a hook behind the door and put our cases in the corner.

'Settle yourselves at the table,' Mr Hollingsworth told us, as he filled the teapot and poured four mugs of tea.

'Thanks, Mr Hollingsworth,' I smiled.

'Thank you, Mr Hollingsworth,' said Freddie.

But the old man tapped his finger on the table and leaned across to us. 'Now, before we go any further,' he said, 'how would you feel about calling me Arthur, eh? Everybody does.'

Dad tried to protest, but Arthur wouldn't have it. He lifted his hand and shook his head. 'It's what I want. It would please me if you called me Arthur.'

So after that, we did.

'Does everybody have a house like yours, Arthur?' asked Freddie as he stared at the carpets on the wall.

Arthur smiled. 'Not exactly like this,' he said, taking a mouthful of tea. 'Some are bigger. Some are smaller. Some are made of brick and stone. Whatever people can find.'

'Basil lives in a railway carriage, doesn't he?' I said.

'He does,' said Arthur, wiping his mouth with a red spotted handkerchief. 'And very nice it is too.'

'I've never seen a place like Whiteway,' I told him. 'I've only lived in Rochdale.'

'Ah, Whiteway's special all right,' he said, leaning forward and tapping his nose as if he was telling us a secret, just like Dad did. 'It were started years ago by anarchists. Know what them are?'

'No. What are they?'

'I'll tell you, Lizzie,' said Arthur, lowering his voice. 'Anarchists don't believe in the law, see.'

This was interesting. I wondered if Podgy Watson was an anarchist. He had broken most of our school rules.

'Not believing in the law is bad, isn't it?' I asked.

'Depends,' said Arthur. 'You see, the anarchists didn't have no truck with governments and being told what to do. But people at Whiteway help each other – and people like your dad.'

'You mean, they agree with Dad about not going to war?'

'Oh, ah,' he said. 'We have conscientious objectors here, and others who escaped from the Nazis or fled from the Spanish Civil War. We welcome everybody, see? We don't have no rules here, Lizzie.'

That sounded fantastic to me, but just when I thought everything was going brilliantly, Dad interrupted to say that he had to make a rule just for us.

'That's not fair,' we chorused. But no matter how much we stamped our feet and wailed, Dad insisted.

This was his rule: we were not allowed to go out of Whiteway. Not even into the nearest village.

'Why not?' I asked.

'Listen,' said Arthur, taking hold of my hand. 'Miserden isn't far away. It's a small place where everybody knows everybody. They'll spot that you're new round here and they'll guess where you live, see.'

'I don't understand. What's wrong with that?'

'The police would put two and two together and come and arrest me, Lizzie,' said Dad. 'That's what's wrong.' I slumped onto a chair, feeling miserable until Dad added, 'So, you won't be able to go to school.'

All at once, things looked brighter. *No school!* No bullies like Podgy Watson, or teachers like Miss Rossendale. No spelling tests. No maths homework.

Things were getting better and better.

'Where's your bedroom, Arthur?' Freddie asked. 'Haven't you got one?'

'I sleep over there,' he said, pointing to what looked like a settee without arms. He had put a cover and some cushions on his mattress and I guessed he must use it as a seat during the day.

Freddie frowned and looked around, puzzled. Then he tugged on Arthur's sleeve. 'But what about us? Are we going to sleep with you in your bed?'

'No, son,' Arthur laughed. 'You've got your own.'

'I can't see it,' Freddie said.

'Ah!' Arthur winked at him. 'It's hidden away.' He stood up and walked over to a big cupboard opposite the stove and he opened the door. Inside was a mattress, two pillows and a blue eiderdown.

Freddie squealed and jumped with excitement when he saw it. 'Is it ours, Arthur? Can we really sleep in a cupboard?'

Arthur grinned. 'Think you can fit in?'

He needn't have worried. That night we snuggled up together in our cupboard bed as cosy as kittens. We even made room for Jip, who curled up on our feet so they were all toasty and warm while Dad slept on a rug in front of the stove.

It had been a long day and, as my eyes grew heavy, I wondered if Mum's star was shining over Arthur's house, watching us. 'See you tomorrow, Mum,' I whispered and fell fast asleep.

Seven

We settled into life at Whiteway straight away. When we woke the next morning, Arthur showed us how to get water from the butt to wash our faces, and he pointed out the tin bath hanging on the wall – just like the one we had at home.

'We'll carry it in on Fridays,' Arthur explained, 'and fill it up with hot water from the stove. Once a week, mind. So don't get too mucky! And if we run out of water, you might have to fetch some from the spring on the other side of the road.'

For breakfast, Arthur made us porridge on the stove and spooned it into bowls which he set on the table. Then he dropped a spoonful of honey into each one.

Freddie stirred the golden liquid round and round until it disappeared. 'Where does honey come from?' he asked.

Arthur smiled. 'We've got plenty of bees buzzing about Whiteway, son. Most people round here keep a beehive so that's how we get our honey.'

Beehives and honey! We didn't have those where we came from.

After breakfast, we went behind the house to see the hen coop and the vegetable patch, which stretched almost down to the wood. Arthur let us dig up a cabbage and some parsnips and collect some eggs which we carried back for dinner.

'You can go and get some bread too, if you like,' he said as he started peeling the parsnips.

'Where do we get it from?' asked Freddie.

I knew. 'We passed Protheroe's Bakery near Mrs Weaver's house. I bet that's where you get it from.'

Arthur smiled. 'You're right, Lizzie,' he said and gave us some money and a basket, and we walked down the hill to the shop. We bought a large crusty loaf and it was the best bread we had ever tasted – soft and fluffy in the middle and crisp on the outside. Delicious!

That afternoon, Arthur said, 'Come on. Get your coats and I'll show you round.' He took us for a walk down the paths that criss-crossed Whiteway and pointed out the houses dotted about, sometimes hidden among trees. Jip came with us, too, and he had a fine old time sniffing out rabbits. Every now and then we stopped to talk to people who seemed to know Arthur very well and he introduced us. They were ever so friendly.

'Of course, the children are at school at this time of day,' he said. 'And a lot of folks are out working.'

'What do they do?' asked Freddie.

'Well, there's the clothing factory in Gloucester, or some are in the workshops here doing metalwork and repairing stuff. And they all take turns at helping in the fields,' he said, pointing across the road. 'But the weather's too wet to do any ploughing at the moment.'

The grey clouds which had covered the sky all day suddenly thickened and became darker.

'Looks like rain to me,' said Arthur, and he suggested we went back home and had a cup of tea.

But I didn't want to go inside. 'Can I stay out for a bit longer? I want to explore. If it rains I'll come back straight away.'

Dad smiled. 'Half an hour. I'll take Freddie with me. He's tired.'

'Let Jip come with you, Lizzie,' said Arthur. 'He's never tired.'

When they had gone, I wandered along the footpaths and through the trees, happy to be by myself – though I liked having Jip following behind, wagging his tail. 'This place is magical,' I said to him, but I don't suppose he understood.

There were trees everywhere – along paths and between houses. Some grew in clumps and there were areas of woodland where the birds, perched on the bare branches, filled the air with their song. Even without leaves the trees were beautiful, but my favourite one, I decided, was an old oak not far from Arthur's house. It had wide branches that spread to form a canopy over the ground beneath. I looked around for a stone and when I found a sharp one, I scratched the letter L on the trunk.

'You're my special tree,' I said, laying my hand over the letter, just as raindrops began to fall. 'I'll come back soon.' And I raced back to Arthur's with Jip chasing after me.

*

That night, there was a meeting at the Whiteway Colony Hall.

'It's the usual monthly meeting,' said Arthur. 'Most people go if they can. We discuss problems and what we want to do about them.' It sounded boring to Freddie and me, until we learned that Basil was going. So maybe it wouldn't be too bad.

The Colony Hall was a long low building, and by the time we arrived, it was almost full. People were sitting on rows of metal chairs, chatting and catching up on news. At one end of the hall was a table where two men and a woman were sitting ready with pens in their hands. I couldn't help noticing a white-haired lady on the front row wearing a warm jumper of pink, orange and red stripes. She was talking to the man sitting next to her and, without looking at her needles, she was knitting something purple.

'Is that Mrs Weaver?' I asked Basil, who had come to stand near us.

Basil nodded and grinned.

'Does she always knit?'

'Yes. Except when she's weaving.'

We sat at the back of the hall and waited for the meeting to begin. When it did, it was very boring, just as I thought it would be. We had to sit still while the grown-ups talked about the blackout and then about a waterlogged field and how they were going to drain it. I couldn't wait for it to end.

But after all that, there was a surprise.

The man at the front stood up and said, 'And now we

would very much like to welcome William Butterworth and his children, Lizzie and Freddie, to Whiteway.'

Lots of smiles and clapping all round.

'William is a conscientious objector,' he continued.

People clapped even harder. Most of them cheered. Those nearest to Dad patted him on the back and said, 'Well done!'

The man at the front tapped his wooden hammer on the table for quiet and waited till the clapping died down.

'William was refused the official status of a conscientious objector,' he told everybody, 'and he has come to live with Arthur Hollingsworth. But he has the threat of a prison sentence hanging over him. Because of this, please make sure that you tell no one that he and his children are in Whiteway. The police would soon learn of it.'

A murmur rippled round the room. People turned to their neighbours, frowning and nodding and making comments.

'Now on a happier note,' he said, tapping his hammer again, 'Lizzie and Freddie won't be going to the village school for obvious reasons and so we are looking for a teacher for them.'

What? I sat up in my seat, shocked to hear the announcement. Did we ask for a teacher? No we did *not*! We would like to stay at home, thank you very much. I'm sure Arthur could teach us a thing or two.

'Do we have any volunteers?' the man said, looking round the room.

'I would be happy to teach mathematics,' said a deep voice in a strange accent, 'and writing, perhaps.'

I looked around and saw a tall man with steel-rimmed glasses and wild hair standing at the far side of the hall.

'Thank you, Professor Elstein,' said the man at the table.

A professor? No! Too clever! I couldn't even keep up with an ordinary teacher. I slumped in my seat and stared at the floor to avoid looking at him.

And if that wasn't enough, someone else volunteered. A dark-haired lady, hardly any taller than I was, stood with her hand in the air. 'I could teach the little boy,' she called out. 'I used to be a teacher in Spain.'

'Excellent. Thank you, Lalia. The problem is solved,' said the man at the front. 'That concludes the business for this evening and we can now enjoy the music of the Brandon Family. Thank you.'

Nobody noticed how miserable I was. They all started stacking the chairs and packing away the table while a man, a woman and a tall boy dressed in black walked in carrying accordions. As their music began, some people stepped onto the floor and started to dance – waltzing and twirling around – while Professor Elstein walked across the room towards Arthur and shook his hand.

'Good of you to help, Professor,' said Arthur, and he beckoned us over. 'This is Lizzie. She's a good girl.'

'Then I shall be delighted to teach her,' he said, shaking my hand.

The professor had nice grey eyes with lots of crinkles at the edges which showed that he smiled a lot and he was not at all grand – so I felt much better.

'I have some work to finish,' he told me. 'But I should be ready to start your lessons in two weeks, I think.'

Two weeks with no school. That didn't sound too bad.

The dark-haired lady came over next, and Arthur smiled and pushed us forward. 'Here are Lizzie and Freddie,' he said.

'How do you do, Lizzie and Freddie. My name is Lalia,' and she smiled and held out her hand, shaking ours in turn.

'Are you going to be my teacher?' asked Freddie.

'I am,' said Lalia, bending her knees so that she could talk to Freddie face to face. 'Would you like that, Freddie?'

He nodded. 'I think so. You look like a nice teacher.'

She laughed and then she stood up and turned to a boy behind her. 'This is my son, Bernardo.'

He was a year or so older than I was – probably thirteen – but he was already several inches taller than his mother, with the same dark hair. I couldn't help noticing that there was a fist-sized bruise on his face and a cut by his mouth.

'I hope you children will be friends,' said Lalia. 'Bernardo is one of those boys who gets into fights at school and he's always in trouble.'

'Mother!' Bernardo growled under his breath and shuffled his feet, embarrassed.

'I don't know what I'm going to do with him,' she sighed. 'So I hope you will be a good influence, Lizzie.'

Dad grinned. 'I hate to disappoint you, Lalia, but I doubt Lizzie will set a good example. She can be quite a handful herself.'

'Dad!' I said, nudging him with my elbow.

But that didn't stop him. 'You see that red hair of hers?' he said, laughing, 'That should tell you she's got a terrible temper.'

It was Dad's idea of a joke, and I didn't think it was very funny, but at least it cheered up Bernardo. When he heard that I wasn't Little Miss Perfect, his eyes lit up. He looked across at me and his mouth twitched into a smile. By the end of that evening, we were the best of friends.

Eight

The one thing I didn't like about sleeping in the cupboard was that it didn't have a window I could look out of. So I didn't see Mum's star the next night, or the one after that. *What if it has vanished?* I thought and I couldn't sleep for worrying about it.

I lay there listening to Arthur's snores from across the room, and Dad, who was sleeping on the floor, was snoring almost as loud. Then I suddenly realised that there was nothing to stop me getting up and going outside now. Nobody would know.

I sat up, put on my glasses and climbed over Freddie. There was a night-light flickering on the table, so I could see my way across the room without tripping over Dad. The door wasn't locked. All I had to do was lift the latch and open it.

I stepped into the January night, with my coat over my nightie. The sky was clear and a moon like a bright white ball hung in midair.

I stood outside Arthur's house, craning my neck, searching for Mum. There were so many stars that night but I found her all right. She was the biggest one and twinkled more than any of the others.

But looking wasn't enough. I needed to talk to her – out loud where no one could hear. I ran along the path that led to my special tree – the old oak with my initial on it – and I sank to the ground, leaning my back against its trunk. Then the words poured out. I told Mum everything that had happened since we left Rochdale. *Everything*. Even the bad bits about the dead sheep. 'I knew you'd want to know, Mum.' I said.

I was almost talked out when I heard a noise. At first I thought it must be a rabbit or a squirrel, but it grew louder until I realised that someone was walking in the wood and the footsteps were heading my way. I tried to stand up, ready to run back to Arthur's, but my legs were stiff with cold and I slipped and crashed to the ground. I must have twisted my ankle because it hurt like mad and I moaned quite a bit.

I sat there rubbing the pain away and when I looked up I was surprised to see Bernardo standing there, staring at me.

'Are you all right?' he said.

I nodded and rubbed some more.

'Who were you talking to?' he asked.

'My mum,' I said, looking up at the sky. 'That's her.' And I explained all about the star and how a bomb had fallen on her shop by mistake because the pilot had probably got the wrong map.

'That's bad luck,' he said, sitting on the ground next to me. 'Papá was killed by a bomb too – when I was little.'

'In London?'

'No, in Guernica.'

It turned out that Guernica was in Spain. No wonder I hadn't heard of it, because I'd never been to Spain. Bernardo didn't know why they bombed the town, but I wondered if Spanish pilots had problems with maps too.

'After Papá died we had no food,' he said, 'and bombs were falling all the time. Mamá heard there was a ship that was going from Bilbao, the nearest port, to England so we walked for days until we reached it. There were four thousand kids packed on that ship, and the sea was so rough that we were all seasick.'

'Poor you. So you both came to Whiteway?'

'No. First we had to stay in horrible tents near the beach and it was very cold. They made me drink some stuff called Horlicks and I hated it. I threw it away and got into terrible trouble. But Mamá didn't care.'

'What happened?'

'A lady came who was very kind and didn't make me drink Horlicks. She brought us here. That was nearly five years ago but I still miss Papá.'

We sat for a while not saying anything. I guess Bernardo was thinking about his dad and I was thinking about my mum.

'So why aren't you in bed?' I asked him.

'I often come here,' he said. 'But Mamá doesn't like it when I'm out after dark. She told me not to do it so I'll get into trouble if she finds me gone.'

'What if she sees that your bed's empty?'

Bernardo snorted. 'She won't – but I'll take the risk. I want to see the bombers.'

'What bombers? I thought we were in the country.'

He looked up at the sky. 'See that moon?' he said.

I nodded.

'They call it a bomber's moon, because the pilots can see their targets easily when it's shining like that. The Jerry planes are sure to come over tonight. They might go for Bristol. The docks or the aircraft factories, maybe.' Bernardo stood up. 'If you want to get a good view, we'll have to climb this tree. Come on. I've done it before.'

I shook my head. 'I've got to go. Dad might wake up and see that I'm not in bed.'

'Typical girl,' grunted Bernardo. 'No sense of adventure. You go home to Daddy then, but I'm going to watch the planes.'

He put his foot on the lowest bough, then looked back at me and grinned. 'I bet you're scared of climbing, aren't you, Lizzie? Most girls are.'

Well, that did it. I'd show him that I could climb as well as any boy. I jumped to my feet and stepped onto a strong branch, pulling myself from one to the next as Bernardo climbed ahead of me. Once I'd reached the top, I straddled a thick branch and clung on. The moon was so bright that you could see fields, houses, farms, everything. It felt like you could see to the other side of the world.

We hadn't been up there long before I heard a siren some way off. It was a terrible, scary wailing noise.

'We'd better go into a shelter,' I said. 'That's what we do at home.'

45

Bernardo shook his head. 'Nobody bothers about the sirens in Whiteway,' he said. 'They never drop bombs round here, see.'

I was surprised. I knew for a fact that Jerry pilots sometimes dropped bombs in the wrong places. But I didn't worry cos Dad was probably sleeping. He snores really loud, so I bet he hadn't even heard the siren. That's what I told myself anyway.

'If we're lucky, we'll see the planes from up here,' Bernardo said, pointing into the distance where searchlights were beaming into the sky. At first they were yellow, but he explained that it took them time to warm up and they'd soon get stronger and brighter.

When they did, they looked like brilliant pencils of light, searching for the Jerry planes, turning this way and that. It was really exciting. We were ready for them!

'When will they come, Bernardo?'

'Listen,' he said, cocking his ear. 'They're coming now.'

As I clung onto the branch, I heard a distant drone which grew louder. I held my breath. I only saw one plane at first, but there were others behind it. Plane after plane.

'Luftwaffe!' Bernardo shouted. 'They're here. See, I told you.'

My heart was racing. I'd never seen a raid before and I wasn't sure that I wanted to now. Then something fell from the first plane – blue stars which hung in the sky before suddenly bursting into bright lights.

'What's happening?'

'Flares. He's lighting up the target so the other planes can drop their bombs. But our gunners will get 'em, just wait. They'll shoot 'em down. Any minute now, Lizzie.'

We were sitting there watching the drama when the big guns sounded – probably in Stroud, Bernardo said. They started thrumping and walloping, aiming at the planes. It was very loud even though it was miles away. *Bang, bang, bang!*

That was why I didn't hear Lalia. It was only when I looked down that I saw her at the bottom of the tree, shouting with her hands cupped round her mouth.

We were in serious trouble.

'Bernardo!' we finally heard. 'Come down. What have I told you about wandering around at night?'

Bernardo called to her. 'All right. I'm coming.'

Then she shouted, 'Who is up there with you? Both of you get down at once.'

So we had to climb out of the oak tree – we never did see the Jerry planes shot down.

When we landed at Lalia's feet, I could see she was shaking with anger. She used words like 'dangerous', 'irresponsible' and 'foolish'.

My ankle was still throbbing as she marched me back to Arthur's house where things got even worse. Freddie was awake and in floods of tears. Arthur was awake too and trying to quieten Freddie. And Dad was out looking for me.

'He thought you'd run away, my girl,' said Arthur. 'Ever so upset he was. Not nice, Lizzie.'

I felt bad. I went and stood in the doorway and called, 'Dad! I'm here,' into the darkness until I saw him come running up the path with a torch in his hand, his face screwed up with worry.

I didn't mean to upset him.

I glanced at the sky, hoping Mum's star would make me feel better, but it was hidden behind a small cloud. I guessed she was cross with me too.

Nine

By the following week, Freddie had started his lessons with Lalia, and Dad was out repairing farm machinery at the workshop.

'It's hard work, Lizzie,' he said before he went. 'But it's important to keep those old machines working on the land. Without them, we wouldn't grow so much wheat or potatoes – and food is scarce enough.'

Bernardo went to school in Miserden village, so he was away all day and I felt lonely and bored. Arthur did his best to keep me occupied. I helped dig the veg patch and repair the hen coop and fencing. 'Got to keep that old fox away from the chickens,' Arthur explained.

Then one morning, we came back home for a cup of tea and found a note pushed under the door. Arthur picked it up and read it. 'Very good!' he said, passing it over to me. 'The professor's coming over this afternoon to see about your lessons, Lizzie.'

Should I be pleased or should I be scared? My fluttering stomach told me I was nervous – *very* nervous. The professor was a genius, according to Arthur, and I was pretty terrible in the brains department. *What if his kind of sums were miles more difficult than Miss Rossendale's?*

He arrived at two o'clock, stooping as he walked through

the door, wrapping his long black coat across his chest. His hair, which had been blown about by the wind, looked wilder than ever and his glasses had slipped to the end of his nose.

'Good afternoon,' he said, nodding at Arthur and putting an exercise book onto the table.

The butterflies in my stomach multiplied and some flew down to my knees and started them knocking.

But then he said, 'I hope I'm not late, Lizzie. I'm not the best timekeeper in the world.' And he smiled a smile so wide that it spread from one ear to the other. That beautiful smile melted my butterflies and all of a sudden I felt really cheery.

'Now, young lady,' he said as he took off his coat and sat at the table. 'I would like to discuss what kind of mathematics you would like to learn.'

I was amazed. No one had ever asked me a question like that before. 'I don't know,' I replied. 'I never understood sums. I never knew why I had to do them. It's not like reading, is it?'

The professor looked at me and winked, which surprised me because I didn't know that brainy people ever winked. 'I see I shall have to teach you how useful sums can be.' He turned to Arthur. 'I believe you have a building planned, Arthur. Is that right?'

Arthur looked almost as surprised as me. 'Er…yes,' he said. 'But we haven't told the children yet.'

'Then perhaps you should.'

'What is it, Arthur? What building?'

He stroked his beard. 'Well,' he said, pulling up a chair, 'your dad and me are planning to build a room onto the back of the house. We thought you should have a proper bedroom, see.'

'With a window?'

'Yes, with a window.'

I leaped up from my chair and flung my arms around his neck. 'Oh thank you, Arthur,' I said. 'That will be great. I'll be able to see the stars.'

'Ah,' said the professor, 'so you are interested in astronomy?'

I nodded, but I didn't say anything about Mum in case he didn't understand.

'So,' Professor Elstein said, 'this building project will be excellent for you, Lizzie.'

'Will it?' I asked. I couldn't see what the new bedroom had got to do with sums.

'It will,' he answered, opening the exercise book. We will take the measurements and do some drawings, and tomorrow you can come to my house and we will start to work out what we will need.'

'It'll depend on what Basil can get,' said Arthur but the professor waved his hand. 'Ya, ya. I know that. But Lizzie will soon learn how useful mathematics can be.'

Later, when Dad came back home, I ran down the path to meet him. 'Dad! Arthur's going to build us a bedroom!'

Dad laughed and swung me around in a circle like he used to do when I was little. 'I know,' he said. 'We were keeping it a secret until we'd talked to Basil. He's the one who'll have to find us the building materials.'

'And the professor is teaching me how to work things out,'

I told him. 'So we know how much stuff we need. I start my lessons tomorrow.'

'Excellent,' smiled Dad. 'We should go and see Basil. I think he's at home. I saw his lorry.'

We walked over to Basil's railway carriage that evening. Just Dad and me and Freddie. Arthur stayed at home. He'd been suffering with his chest and was coughing a lot, so he wanted to rest. 'I'll be all right. You go,' he said.

This was the first time we had been inside Basil's home. He was a very busy man, always out and about fetching and carrying for people.

He saw us coming down the path and flung open the door, shouting, 'Welcome! Marvellous to see you all. Come in. Come in.'

We climbed up the steps into the carriage, which was very long — like three caravans stuck end to end. There were windows all the way down both sides of the narrow room and below them was wood panelling.

'I like your house,' said Freddie, and he went to sit on one of the bench seats, which were upholstered in red plush and set on either side of a table.

Further down the carriage there were shelves filled with books. Two comfy chairs were set by a stove that was round and black and had a pipe coming out of the top, taking the smoke out through the carriage roof.

'That's my bedroom through there, don't you know?' Basil pointed to a door at the far end. 'Go and take a look while I put the kettle on.'

'Yes please!' said Freddie, jumping off the seat and running down the carriage. We opened the door and stepped into another long thin room. The walls had windows on each side, and there was a small wooden chest and a narrow bed covered by a wool bedspread with multicoloured stripes. 'Do you think Mrs Weaver made that?' I whispered to Freddie and he nodded.

Basil's home was like a magical fairytale. Everything was small and neat and beautiful.

'Can we live in a railway carriage?' Freddie shouted as he ran back into Basil's living room. 'Can we, Dad? Can we?'

Dad shook his head. 'But maybe you'll ride in a train one day.'

We told Basil about the plans for the bedroom and I gave him the drawing I had made with the professor's help. 'Hmm, very good, Lizzie. Very clear.'

'We need wood or bricks, Basil,' said Dad. 'Any chance of getting some?'

'I think you could be in luck, old boy. I've just heard about some bomb damage that might have thrown up something useful. Gloucester way. Plenty of wood, don't you know?'

'Could you get it for us?' Dad asked. 'Do you have the petrol?'

Basil nodded. 'I could go on Saturday. Bernardo will come to give me a hand. He's a strong chap.'

So that was how we left it, but I couldn't help envying Bernardo. He was going out with Basil while I had to stay put in Whiteway.

*

Bernardo and I had arranged to meet in the wood a few days later on Friday. We often did when he was home from school. Sometimes we went down to the pool on the edge of Whiteway or we just messed about climbing trees.

'How did you get on with the professor?' he asked.

'Good. I'm learning how to work out what materials we need for the new bedroom.'

'Basil told me about that.'

'I never thought mathematics could be so useful. Professor Elstein says that people who design buildings—'

'You mean architects?'

'Yes, architects. Well, they use mathematics a lot. I like the professor. He's not at all bossy and he listens to me.'

We walked up to the pool and stood by the edge, skimming pebbles into the water.

'I'm going with Basil tomorrow to help him fetch some wood.'

'You don't have to tell me. I know,' I said peevishly, kicking the soil on the footpath. 'You get to do all the exciting things.'

Bernardo turned and looked at me. 'Why don't you come then? What's stopping you?'

'What do you think's stopping me?' I snapped. 'I'm not allowed to go outside of Whiteway, am I?'

He flicked a stone to the far side of the pool and watched it drop into the water. 'That's just stupid. You don't have to hide away for ever. Who's going to know you over near Gloucester? Are they going to say, "Oh look, that girl over there is the daughter of a man the police are looking for? She must be living up at Whiteway. Let's tell the police."'

'That's silly.'

'Yes, it is. And just think how much you could help us. Why not talk to your dad?'

'I don't know, Bernardo.'

'*Talking* won't do any harm. People in Whiteway discuss ideas all the time. Give it a go, Lizzie. Speak to your dad.'

So I did.

'No!' he said straight away. Just like that. 'No!'

'Why not, Dad?'

'You know what you promised, Lizzie.'

Arthur, who had been resting on his bed, sat up. 'Now, now, Will. Let's discuss it. Is it really such a dangerous thing to do?'

'Yes, it certainly is,' said Dad, his face flushing with anger.

Before the argument could continue, Lalia walked in with Freddie. 'Is anything wrong?' she asked. 'I could hear your voices from the bottom of the path.'

So we told her.

'Is this such a problem?' said Lalia, resting her hand on my shoulder. 'I agree with Lizzie. There's nobody in Gloucester who would recognise her. I think it would do her good to get out for an afternoon.'

So it was three against one.

In the end, Dad gave me one of his looks and said, 'All right then, Lizzie. As long as you're sensible.'

I jumped up and hugged him tight. 'Thanks, Dad. I promise I will be.'

*

Basil was glad to have me along. On Saturday morning we set off as soon as it was light and drove to the outskirts of Gloucester, which had been damaged in an air raid.

'Here we are,' said Basil, turning off the main road and into a street where the houses were not much more than heaps of rubble. It was a real mess, and I wondered if those planes we'd seen over the wood could have dropped their bombs here.

'Poor souls,' Basil sighed and shook his head. 'They've not much left of their homes, have they?' Halfway down, the street was blocked with fallen buildings. Basil jumped out of the cab and walked over to one of the piles. 'We can clear away some of the timber from this end,' he said, pointing to some long pieces of wood. 'Come on then. Let's get cracking, eh?'

We loaded the wood onto the lorry until it was stacked high, and then tied it with rope so that it wouldn't fall off on the way back. Though it was heavy work, I had a great time with Basil and Bernardo. It felt so good to get away from Whiteway for a while. Dad was probably worrying about me all day, but nothing went wrong and I got back safely with just a few splinters and a tear in my skirt.

'Well, if that's all,' said Dad, 'I reckon you had a good day.' And he hugged me.

'Can I go again?' I asked. 'We need lots more stuff for the bedroom.'

I had to beg and plead just like before but he let me go in the end. I went to Gloucester three times and nothing bad happened.

*

The months passed. The weather grew warmer. Dad and Arthur started building the bedroom, and it was amazing to see it grow bit by bit. When it was done we decorated it by dipping sponges into a pot of blue paint and dabbing them on the walls to make a pattern.

Then we threw a party when it was finished. Arthur set a table outside and poured some of his best home-brewed cider into glasses. Lots of people came to celebrate, and Dad made a speech.

'First, I must thank you all for making me and the children so welcome here and most especially for all your support while we've been building,' he said, raising his glass. 'Alan Forester made two fine beds and Mrs Weaver made some splendid blue curtains and Betty Hollinder passed on a marvellous old carpet to keep our toes warm.' Then he turned to Basil. 'We all know Basil. What would we do without him, eh?' Everybody agreed. 'Finding that big window with the glass still in it was nothing short of a miracle. And as for all the corrugated iron for the roof... Well!'

'No problem, old chap,' said Basil, raising his glass. 'Bernardo and Lizzie were a great help.'

Everybody cheered and the bedroom was declared officially open.

That first night in our new room, I was too excited to sleep. I pulled back the curtains and looked up at the stars. 'What do you think, Mum?' I said. 'We did a good job, didn't we?'

Mum's star twinkled and I knew she thought we had.

Ten

In many ways, the war hardly touched us at Whiteway. We helped plough the fields and scatter seeds for new crops. We collected the eggs and saw the vegetables sprouting in their patch.

Newspaper headlines told us how the war had spread all over the world. Arthur pinned a map on the wall and showed us where Germany was, and France and Poland. He pointed out Africa too, where they were having a war in the desert. But I wasn't keen on maps, so I didn't pay much attention.

The worst bit of the war for us was rationing. Clothes were rationed as well as food and I had soon grown out of everything I had brought with me. But Lalia went into Stroud and got clothes from a shop run by the Women's Royal Voluntary Service. They didn't always fit but she was brilliant at altering them.

In late July, just a week before my twelfth birthday, Bernardo said, 'I've got an idea. Are you up for something really exciting?'

'Like what?'

'Something special. But you can't tell your dad. Keep it a secret.'

I didn't trust Bernardo, even though he was my best friend. He liked breaking rules. It could mean trouble.

'Why can't I tell Dad? What is it?'

'There's a fair in Stroud on your birthday. We should go. It'll be fun.'

'I'm not supposed to, Bernardo. You know that.'

'We went to Gloucester loads of times, didn't we?'

'Yes, but Dad knew about that.'

'But nothing terrible happened, did it?'

'I suppose not. But will Basil be going with us?'

'No, dizzy-brain. Where's the adventure in that? We'll go by ourselves. We can use Mum's bike. You ride piggyback. It's only six or seven miles.'

I shook my head. I knew I shouldn't leave Whiteway – Dad would be furious. 'But I don't have any money. What would be the point?'

'I've got a bit,' he said. 'We don't need much. We can have fun just watching.'

'I'm not sure, Bernardo.'

'That means no, I suppose.' He stood in front of me, his hands on his hips. 'Don't you want to have a good time on your birthday? Are you just going to do as you're told and stay at home and do nothing?'

He made me sound stupid. Like a little kid. As if I couldn't make my own decisions. So I said, 'All right then. I'll go. But we've got to get back before anybody misses us.'

That was what we planned and I really didn't think anything bad would come of it.

On the morning of my birthday there were presents waiting for me – a wooden chair which Dad had made, a picture drawn by Freddie and a fantastic surprise from Arthur. He handed me a cardboard box and when I opened the lid I saw there was a tiny yellow chick inside.

'If you look after her proper,' he told me, 'she'll give you plenty of eggs for your breakfast.'

'Oh, I will and I think I'll call her Henny Penny.'

Then Arthur squeezed a half-crown into my hand. 'Put that somewhere safe, Lizzie. Save up for when this war is over and you'll have things to spend it on.'

'We're having a special tea this afternoon,' Dad said at breakfast. 'Lalia has been saving up her butter rations and she's baking a cake as a special treat.'

'We'll have a real spread,' agreed Arthur.

I was thrilled to bits. 'What a great birthday! Thanks for everything.'

Dad didn't go to the workshop that morning and Freddie didn't have lessons because it was summer now and the other children were on holiday. All four of us went into the wood and built a den. It was small, just big enough for two or three people, and we covered it with bracken so you could hardly see it was there.

'Perfect for bird-watching,' said Arthur.

'Perfect,' I nodded. 'I've never had a proper den made out of branches. We always used the clotheshorse and a sheet at home.'

When we'd finished, we headed back to Arthur's house. 'What time is it, Dad?' I asked.

'Are you going somewhere?'

'I promised to meet Bernardo at eleven o'clock.'

Dad looked at his watch. 'Then you'd better get off, love,' he said. 'Make sure you're back for half past four. Don't want the birthday girl to miss her party!'

I hurried down the path, waving goodbye as I went, feeling Arthur's half-crown jangling in my pocket.

But Freddie came running after me. 'Where are you going, Lizzie?'

I turned and told him to go back. 'Stop following me, Freddie.'

'No,' he said. 'Tell me where you're going.'

Now he was six, he was very stubborn and didn't always do as he was told.

'I'm going over the fields,' I lied.

'Can I come with you?'

'No, Freddie. Go back.'

'Why can't I?' he whined. 'Why do I have to stay behind? I *always* have to stay behind. It's not fair.'

His face scrunched up as if he would burst into tears at any minute. So I tried to explain. 'You can't come because it's *my* birthday and I'm going on an adventure.'

'What adventure?'

'It's a secret.'

'I won't tell anybody. '

I sighed. 'I bet you will. I bet you'll go and tell Dad.'

'No. No, I won't,' he said. His eyes filled with tears that spilled onto his cheeks. 'I can keep a secret. Please, Lizzie. Tell me.'

I shouldn't have told him, but I couldn't bear to see him upset. So I said, 'I'm going with Bernardo to Stroud.'

'Is that a long way?'

'No not really but I don't want Dad to worry. That's why it's a secret. I'll be back for tea.'

'Oh,' he said, wiping his face with the back of his hand, 'that's all right then cos we're having a party, with cake and everything.'

'And if you keep the secret, I might bring you something from Stroud.'

Freddie's face lit up at the thought of a present. 'Thanks, Lizzie,' he said. 'I won't tell. I promise.'

He raced back up the hill and I hurried down to where Bernardo was waiting by the horse chestnut tree with Lalia's old black bike at his side.

'You're sure your mum won't miss this, Bernardo?'

'Course she won't. She's too busy baking today.' He pushed the bike onto the path and swung his leg over the crossbar. 'Come on. I'll ride standing up. You sit on the saddle.'

I held onto his shoulders while I settled onto the bike and we headed off, wobbling at first. We were on our way!

We rode down the lane and onto the main road.

'This is Miserden village,' Bernado shouted over his shoulder as we passed a group of houses with low stone walls, and a post office with its blind pulled across to shade the window from the sun. 'Look over there,' he pointed to the right. 'That's my school.'

We rode on with the midday sun beating on our heads. By the time we reached Stroud we were hot and very thirsty and drank from a water fountain before walking across to the field where the fair had set up.

'We'll have to leave at three o'clock,' I said. 'I've got to be back by tea time, remember?'

'I know, I know,' he said. 'Come on. Let's go and enjoy ourselves.'

We had just walked into the fairground when somebody called out, 'What *you* doin' here?'

I turned round to see two boys leaning against a fence. One had greasy black hair and wore a checked shirt and the other was small and skinny with a thin, pale face.

Bernardo looked at them, his mouth tightened. 'What do you *think* we're doing here?' he snapped. 'Same as you, of course.'

The black-haired boy sneered and walked over. 'Foreigners ain't allowed in fairgrounds. Didn't you know that, dago?'

'I'm Spanish – not *dago*! And that's rich, coming from you. Calling people names. It's not as if you belong round here. You're evacuees. So why don't you go back to London, eh?'

It turned out that the boys were in Bernardo's class at Miserden School. They had been billeted with an old couple in the village to escape the bombing.

They were now standing face to face. The mousy one snarled and pushed Bernardo's shoulder. 'Why don't you go back to dago land, then? Nobody likes you lot from Whiteway. Everybody thinks you're weird.'

The other one laughed. Bernardo flexed his fingers and I could see that a fight was coming – so I grabbed his arm. 'Come on. Let's go. Leave 'em to it.' And I dragged him away.

'That's right,' the boys called after him. 'Let your girlfriend tell you what to do.' And they stood there shaking with laughter as we walked away.

I could feel Bernardo tense and he gritted his teeth, but I gripped his arm tighter. 'Leave the bike there,' I said, 'and let's go and enjoy ourselves. It's my birthday, remember.'

Bernado took the bike round the back of a caravan, glancing over his shoulder at the two boys who were now pulling faces at him. Finally they lost interest, stuffed their hands in their pockets and walked off.

Eleven

'Did I tell you Arthur gave me half-a-crown for my birthday?'
I said as we went around the funfair. I felt a bit guilty. I was
supposed to save it for something special – but the funfair
was special, wasn't it?

'That's great!' said Bernardo, cheering up already. 'I've got
three shillings. What shall we spend our money on?'

We walked round but couldn't decide. Should it be the big
wheel? Or the bumper cars? Or the shooting range?

'The coconuts are the cheapest,' said Bernardo. 'Thrupence
for three balls.' We agreed we should start there.

Bernardo went first. His aim wasn't good and he missed
the coconuts by a mile, which made me laugh. 'Bet you
can't do any better,' he sulked. 'Girls are useless at
throwing.'

'Watch me,' I said as I picked up my three balls. 'I'll show
you.' I did, too. I knocked three coconuts off the stands. 'Got
'em!' I yelled. 'I can take one home for Freddie. I promised
him a present.'

We went from stall to stall carrying the coconut. We had
soon spent most of our money until we went on the roll-a-
penny. I won a shilling and Bernardo won sixpence. This
meant we still had enough for a ride on the bumper cars.

'Come on!' said Bernardo. 'Let's have a go.'

I had never been on one before — but it looked really exciting. Bashing and bumping. People laughing and screaming.

We joined the queue, waiting for the next ride, and were shuffling forward towards the pay kiosk when we heard a familiar voice. It was the dark-haired boy in the checked shirt. 'Oh look,' he called. 'It's dago boy and his girlfriend.'

My heart sank. Bernardo's least favourite people were in the queue not far behind us.

'Who's your girlfriend?' shouted the small boy with the pale face.

'I'm not his girlfriend,' I called back. 'Leave us alone.'

'*Ooooh!* The little girl's got a temper!'

'Shut it!' Bernardo said. 'And don't call her little. She's loads taller than you.'

This stupid argument ended when we reached the kiosk and paid our money.

Ignoring the two boys, we ran over to the far side of the rink. Clutching the coconut I jumped into a red bumper car as Bernardo leaped into a blue one. The boys climbed together into a black car.

'Hey, you two! You'd better watch out!' they yelled — we knew what to expect.

Once everybody was seated, the man in charge of the ride flicked a switch and the cars started to move. I swung mine round and got as far away from the boys as I could, but it was Bernardo they were after.

CRASH!

66

'Gotcha!' shouted the boy in the checked shirt.

Bernardo's car went spinning backwards and before he could turn in their direction, they came at him again.

CRASH!

Bernardo was helpless. Stuck in a corner. No matter how frantically he turned the steering wheel, the car wouldn't move. The boys were already backing away, ready to charge at him again.

CRASH!

'How does that feel?' yelled the taller one, standing up in the car and balling his fist. But I was already heading over to Bernardo. They didn't see me coming. My turn!

CRASH!

I hurtled into their car at full speed, knocking the boy off balance and sending the black car whizzing away from Bernardo. Before they could gain control, I crashed into them again, by which time Bernardo had managed to move his car away from the side. Now it was two cars against one. Bernardo rammed the black car from one side and I rammed it from the other until the two boys were shaken so badly that, when the ride finally came to an end, they climbed out and staggered to the side like a pair of drunken sailors.

'We'll get you, toerag,' one shouted over his shoulder.

'Will you?' Bernardo called back.

'Yeah. You'll be sorry.'

Bernardo was about to run after them so I stepped in front of him, refusing to move until he calmed down. 'Take no notice,' I said and we took our time, walking across the bumper car ride towards the steps at the other side. As we reached the bottom, I glanced at the clock above the pay kiosk and was shocked to see that it was quarter to four. 'We're late! We'll never make it back in time.'

Bernardo didn't seem worried. 'We'll ride faster, that's all. Come on.'

We pushed through the crowds, past the coconut shy and over to the caravan to collect the bike.

But the bike wasn't there. I couldn't believe it. 'It's gone,' I said. 'Someone must have taken it.'

Bernardo's face flushed red. 'And I can guess who. Those two worms have got it.' He looked towards the entrance, standing on tiptoe to see over the heads of the crowd. 'They're over there,' he said, pointing ahead. 'Come on.'

We forced our way through the people still flocking to the fair. Luckily, the two boys were even slower than we were because they had the bike with them. We had almost caught up when the dark-haired one turned round and spotted us.

Bernardo yelled at him. 'Hey! That's my bike!' People in the crowds looked at us, and the boys knew the game was up. They flung it on the ground and the smaller boy ran off. But the other one didn't. He had something he wanted to do first. He looked at us, smirking, before he jumped with all his force on the front wheel – once, twice, three times.

Then he ran away, laughing and shouting, 'See ya!'

When we examined the bike, we found that the spokes were smashed and the rim of the wheel had buckled.

'It's ruined,' I groaned. 'What will Lalia say?'

'Let's not think about that,' said Bernardo. 'We'd better start walking.'

'It'll take hours. I'll be late for the party and Dad'll go crazy.'

The bike was ruined. My birthday was ruined and I was in serious trouble. And to top it all, I'd lost Freddie's coconut.

The road to Whiteway stretched on and on in front of us. The crooked wheel wobbled and pushing the bike was hard work, slowing us down. My shoes rubbed blisters on my heels and my legs ached like never before. But we kept going and by the time we reached the far side of Miserden, we were exhausted, hot and thirsty.

'It's no good,' I said. 'I'll have to stop for a bit.'

'Me too,' agreed Bernardo and we sat on the grass verge at the side of the road. It was then that a lorry came along heading in the direction of Stroud. We didn't take much notice until we realised it was Basil's lorry. Then we jumped up and waved like mad to attract his attention. As soon as he saw us, he screeched to a halt and wound down the window.

'Lizzie! Bernardo!' he shouted. 'Where have you been?'

I limped across the road. 'You don't know how good it is to see you, Basil,' I called up to him. 'Will you give us a lift back home, please? We're really late for my birthday party.'

'Right,' he said. 'Put the bike in the back.'

'Come on, Bernado,' I called. 'Basil's going to take us home.'

But as Bernardo picked up the bike and pushed it towards

the lorry, someone jumped down from the passenger's side. I couldn't see who it was at first until I came face to face with him.

It was Dad.

I had never seen him so furious. He was shaking with anger and I was terrified.

He pointed his finger at me. 'You broke your promise. You left Whiteway. How could you? You know what that could mean.'

I tried to explain but he wouldn't listen.

'Lalia made you a special birthday tea and you didn't arrive. I was out of my mind with worry, wondering where you were,' he said, his voice getting louder and louder. 'If Freddie hadn't eventually told me you'd gone to Stroud, I wouldn't have had any idea where to look for you.'

While Dad was shouting, an old man peered over his garden wall. 'What's all the fuss? Everythin' all right, boy?'

Dad turned and held up his hand. 'Aye. It's these two. They went missing. Been to the fair without us knowing.'

'Ah,' said the man, waving his hand. 'Kids, eh?' And he disappeared back behind the stone wall.

Dad told us to get onto the lorry sharpish. 'How dare you take Lalia's bike without asking?' he said as he lifted it over the side. 'It'll need repairing when we get back. How did you get it in that state?'

Without waiting for an answer, he climbed into the cab next to Basil and slammed the door with the terrible force of his anger.

I slumped in the back of the lorry next to Bernardo, my head hung low.

I wished I hadn't gone to the fair.

I wished I hadn't broken my promise.

But it was too late.

Twelve

On the night of my birthday, I went to bed in disgrace. No party. No fun. No nothing. Could things get any worse, I wondered?

Well, they did.

The next morning, as I walked to Protheroe's Bakery, I saw a policeman riding up the main road on an old black bike. There was nothing unusual about that. Nothing to worry about that is until he turned along the path that led to Whiteway.

I raced back home, and by the time I burst through the door my heart was beating at a hundred miles an hour. Arthur was sitting at the table mending an old pan.

'A policeman's coming!' I said, gasping for breath.

'Is that right?' Arthur replied, calm as you like, and he put the pan on the table and stood up. 'I expect it's nowt, Lizzie. He's probably checking the blackout regulations.'

My stomach was churning and my hands were sticky with sweat. 'He might be after my dad,' I said.

'Then he'll be looking for a long time, won't he?' Arthur put his hand on my shoulder. 'Go and get your dad from the workshop, Lizzie. Tell him to go into the wood and stay there.'

'What about Freddie?' I asked. 'He's over with Lalia.'

'Then you'll have to look sharp. Fetch Freddie afterwards, and mind that bobby doesn't see you. I'll come down to the wood when he's gone.'

I left Arthur leaning against the doorframe puffing on his pipe as if he was simply taking the morning air – really he was keeping his eyes open for the visitor.

Luckily for us, the policeman was old and overweight and took ages to cycle up the hill. Then he must have gone knocking on doors, asking questions, until he came to Arthur's house. By that time the three of us were safe inside our hideout in the wood.

'That policeman will be asking around about us,' said Dad as we squeezed in together.

'But Arthur said he's only here to check the blackout.'

Dad shook his head. 'We've been lucky so far, Lizzie,' he said, 'but I've got a bad feeling about today.'

'I like it in here,' smiled Freddie. 'This is exciting. Can we make a fire?'

I wished I could be as cheerful as Freddie. But my head was throbbing and my stomach had tightened into knots. I closed my eyes, trying to hold back terrible thoughts of what had happened yesterday. I tried to hide them. Push them away. Forget them. And when I couldn't do that anymore, I had to tell Dad. 'It's my fault,' I confessed. 'Some boys saw Bernardo and me in Stroud. They knew we lived at Whiteway. They must have told the police.'

Dad patted my hand. 'Why would they know who your dad was?' he said, but by then I was sobbing so he wrapped his arms around me and kissed my forehead. 'Sssh. I don't know who gave us away, Lizzie.'

The wait for Arthur seemed like for ever but at last he peered into our hideaway. 'All clear. You can come back now.' And we crawled out.

'That was good,' said Freddie. 'I like hiding in our den – except when Lizzie cries. Can we do it again tomorrow?'

'Maybe, son. We'll see, eh?'

Arthur gave Dad a funny look. 'It's not good, Will,' he said, lowering his voice so we wouldn't hear. But I did. Every word.

'What did he say, Arthur?' Dad asked.

'Somebody went down to the police station this morning and reported seeing you. Said he'd seen a fella who was young enough and fit enough to be fighting at the front. Said he had two kids with him.'

'Could be that old man who spoke to us yesterday,' said Dad.

'Well, whoever he was,' Arthur replied, 'he thought you must be staying at Whiteway. They recognised Basil and the lorry, see. It's well-known around these parts,' he sighed. 'He said you might be a deserter on the run.'

Arthur's face was grey with worry. 'I did my best,' he said, staring at the ground and shaking his head. 'I told that bobby there weren't nobody with two kids had moved into Whiteway as far as I knew – but he realised I was lying. He saw the nipper's football on the grass. Freddie had marked out a goalpost an' all.'

'I remember,' said Freddie. 'We played yesterday, Dad, and I got ten goals! I'm really good at football, aren't I?'

Arthur smiled and patted Freddie's head. 'Of course you are, mister. Now show me how fast you can run to that tree.'

While Freddie raced off up the path, Arthur turned to Dad and said, 'That bobby went round the back of the house without even asking. I tried to stop him, but he looked through the bedroom window. There was no doubt kids slept in there – what with all those drawings pinned on the wall, and their clothes hanging up. I'm sorry, Will.'

Dad put his hand on Arthur's shoulder. 'So what now?'

'He was a nasty little blighter. I didn't like him at all. Said you couldn't hide for ever.'

'What else?'

Arthur looked so miserable he could hardly speak. 'They're coming tomorrow with a summons.'

When he said that, I felt sick. 'They won't take him away, will they?' I asked.

Dad gripped my shoulders and looked right at me. 'Whatever happens, Lizzie, we're staying together. I promised that before we left home, didn't I? We'll find a way out of this.'

Back at the house, Arthur filled the kettle and while we waited for it to boil, we sat round the table discussing what to do.

'I know,' said Freddie, bouncing up and down with excitement. 'We could live in the hideout. That would be perfick.'

'No, Freddie,' I said. 'It would be freezing cold at night and anyway we didn't make a good job of the roof when we built it. The rain will come in.'

'We could take an umbrella and some food. We'd be like Robin Hood.'

At least it made Dad smile.

We were drinking our tea when Lalia arrived. 'I heard about the policeman,' she said. 'Is it bad news?' and Arthur told her everything.

Then Basil came. 'What did the Old Bill want?' he asked. Arthur repeated the story one more time.

'There is a way out,' Basil said, pouring himself a mug of tea.

'What's that?'

'I know one or two farmer chappies hereabouts. I deliver stuff, don't you know? They're desperate for help on their farms at this time of year. The wheat is ripening fast. It'll soon be harvest time.' He grinned and smoothed his moustache. 'A big strong chap like you, William – I'm pretty sure they'll take you on. They won't care you're on the run.'

'He's right,' said Arthur, 'but someone will have to go and talk to the farmers this afternoon.'

'You can go, can't you, Basil?' said Lalia. 'It won't take long in the lorry.'

But Basil shook his head. 'Sorry, old girl. Haven't got the petrol. Almost used up my ration for this week.'

'Then I'll ride over,' she said, until she remembered what had happened yesterday. 'Oh, I can't. My bicycle is broken.'

I felt a terrible pang of guilt about the bike and my cheeks felt as if they were on fire.

'No problem,' said Arthur. 'I fixed it last night. It weren't that damaged. Nothing that couldn't be mended, any road.'

Basil wrote the names of three farms on a piece of paper and gave it to Lalia. 'I reckon one of these chappies will take him.'

'And the children,' said Dad.

Lalia smiled. 'Of course,' she said, tucking the paper into her pocket. 'You are a family, William. You go together.'

Once she had set off, we packed our suitcases and Arthur said we should go back to the wood. 'You never know with them police fellas. They might just come with their warrant this afternoon. Best stay out of sight.'

Freddie loved the idea of hiding in the wood. He pretended he was Robin Hood and climbed a huge beech tree where he peered through the leaves on the lookout for strangers.

'Do we really have to go?' I asked Dad. 'Can't I say goodbye to the professor? And what about Bernardo? Won't I see him again?'

'I don't know,' said Dad, putting his arm round me. 'Sorry, love.'

Then we just sat there in our hideout and waited for Lalia to come back with news.

Thirteen

We were cramped in there until late in the afternoon, when finally I heard footsteps. 'Somebody's coming,' I said, sitting bolt upright. 'Listen.'

From his position in the beech tree, Freddie yelled, 'Enemy! Enemy!' so that the whole of Whiteway must have heard him.

'It's only me,' Arthur called softly. 'No worries, son.'

Jip was ahead of him, pushing his nose in the shelter, panting noisily and wagging his tail.

Dad shoved the dog away and scrambled through the opening before cupping his hands round his mouth and calling up to Freddie. 'You can stop playing Robin Hood, son. Get down now.'

Freddie gave a whooping noise and scrambled down the tree as if it was all part of his game, while I stood next to Dad, anxious to hear Arthur's news.

'Well, first things first,' he said, putting his hand into his jacket pocket. 'I thought you hideaways might be a bit peckish.' He handed me a small, brown paper package, and when I opened it, I found three cheese sandwiches.

'Thanks,' I said. 'I'm starving.'

'But what about Lalia?' Dad asked. 'Is there any news?'

Arthur nodded. 'Lalia's back.'

'And?'

'She's found somebody who'll have you. She's going to take you there tonight. Don't want folks in the village seeing you leave – somebody might tell the coppers.'

Dad sank onto a tree stump and wiped his forehead with his handkerchief. 'Thank goodness,' he said. 'Thanks, Arthur.'

I bit into a sandwich. 'Where are we going? Is it far away?'

'About nine miles,' said Arthur. 'No neighbours to tell on you. I've met Jacob Carter a few times. Him and his missus will see you right.'

'So I'll be working on the farm?' Dad asked.

Arthur smiled a crooked smile. 'Oh aye, Will. You'll be working right enough. Jacob Carter won't let you slack. He'll make sure you pull your weight.'

Once it had gone dark, we left the wood and went back to Arthur's house. We squeezed as many things as we could into our two suitcases and then we waited for Lalia.

When she arrived, I was glad to see that Bernardo was with her.

'Exciting, eh, Lizzie?' he said. 'Escaping the coppers. Running off in the dark. I'm not missing the fun.'

His mother raised her eyebrows. 'No, Bernardo, I've told you, you're staying here with Arthur until I get back.'

Bernardo's mouth drooped, and so did mine as I suddenly realised we would have to say goodbye. We had had great times together, travelling with Basil, climbing in the woods and getting into trouble. After tonight, who knew when I would see him again?

When it was time to go, Arthur opened the door. 'There's a fine old moon out there,' he said, looking up. 'You'll be able to see your way all right.'

Lalia nodded. 'And I've got a torch if we need it.'

Then Arthur held out his arms and gave Freddie and me a hug.

'I'll miss you, Arthur,' I said, and I bent down to stroke Jip, feeling his warm tongue on the back of my hand.

Bernardo was staring miserably at his feet. 'Right then,' he said. 'See you after the war.'

I nodded and blinked away a tear. 'See you,' I said and turned away.

This was goodbye to Whiteway. As I followed Lalia and Dad, I stared up at the night sky and found Mum's star shining as bright as ever. 'Keep us safe, Mum,' I whispered under my breath. 'Let us find somewhere nice to stay.'

Lalia had already warned us about the village. 'We don't want anyone to see us,' she had said. 'At the bottom of the hill, I think we should climb over the gate into the fields. We can walk behind the hedges until we've passed.'

Walking in the fields was OK – until Freddie slipped in some cow muck and fell over. He screamed blue murder. He couldn't help it. He was only six. Dad grabbed hold of him and told him to shush and dried him off with some dock leaves.

Once we were past the village, we climbed back through the hedge and into the lane. Lalia walked in front of us, pushing her bike.

'How did you find your way this afternoon, Lalia?' said Dad. 'It must have been difficult with no signposts anywhere.'

'Who took them?' Freddie asked.

'Men from the council.'

'Why?'

'It's in case the Germans land.' I told him. 'They wouldn't know where they were, would they?'

'That's a good trick,' said Freddie. 'They'd get lost.'

Once we were well away from the village, Dad said, 'Let's sing. Keep ourselves awake, eh?'

Freddie chose his favourite as usual, 'Run, Rabbit, Run'.

Then we sang Dad's favourite – 'Roll Out The Barrel'.

Then mine, which was 'Hey Little Hen'. But that reminded me that I had left Henny Penny behind and I might never see one of her eggs and I felt sad again.

'Are we nearly there?' Freddie wanted to know. 'I'm tired.'

'It's well past your bedtime, isn't it, little man?' Lalia said, and she let him sit on the saddle of her bike and he nodded off leaning against her. When I was little, Mum used to pick me up and carry me if I was tired. *I miss you, Mum*, I thought as I looked up at the stars.

We kept on walking for ages and ages. My eyelids grew so heavy that, no matter how I tried, I couldn't keep them open. Even my legs were out of control and wobbly. I couldn't walk in a straight line anymore and I soon stumbled off the path and fell into a ditch. It was overgrown with weeds and grass and it felt all soft and lovely. I lay still, breathing in the sweet smell of the earth, wanting to stay there and sleep.

'Lizzie!' Dad called and held out his hand. 'Grab hold, love. Come on, I'll pull you out.'

But I didn't want to move.

'Lizzie!' he called again, and this time he tugged at my coat and I woke.

With Dad's help, I dragged myself from the ditch. Somehow, I stood up. Dad put his arm round me and made sure I stayed awake by talking nonstop.

As light was beginning to break, Lalia said, 'Look, Lizzie. Over there at the top of that hill.' She was pointing to a farmhouse silhouetted against the early morning sky. *Our new home.* I stared at it and suddenly felt wide awake.

'I'll leave you here,' said Lalia when we reached a gate with *Elford Hill Farm* painted on a piece of wood. 'I'll go back now.'

'Stay and rest for a bit,' Dad offered. 'You must be tired.'

'Yes, stay, Lalia,' I said, not wanting her to go.

But she shook her head. 'I'll ride back now. It won't take long. Riding is much quicker than walking.' She lifted Freddie off the saddle. 'We are here, little man,' she said and kissed him awake.

'If you're sure,' said Dad.

'I'm sure,' Lalia replied. Then she spread her arms wide and hugged us one by one, Dad most of all, before she climbed onto her bike and rode away.

Fourteen

When Dad knocked on the door, the sound echoed around the farmhouse. Dogs barked, and a light flickered in one of the bedrooms and then moved downstairs and along the hall. The locks rattled before the door opened and a skinny lady in a blue woollen dressing gown stood in the doorway. She held an oil lamp and two collies danced around her legs making a terrible din.

'You'll be William, I expect,' she called over the noise. 'You'd best come in. Leave your shoes by the door and don't mind the dogs. They won't hurt.' She turned, holding the lamp high, and walked down the hall. We stepped inside and followed her.

'Sorry to disturb you, Mrs Carter,' said Dad. 'We had to come after dark.'

'I knows that,' she said as she led us up the stairs. 'Them young-uns look tired out. Get yourselves a few hours sleep before you come down for breakfast.'

She showed us our bedroom, which was at the top of three flights of stairs, under the eaves. There were two narrow black iron bedsteads, a chair, a chamber pot and a wash stand with a china bowl and a jug of water on it.

Dad cleaned the remains of the cow muck off Freddie's legs before we climbed into bed and curled up together. He tucked the grey blankets round us and he climbed into the other bed. That was the last I remember of that night until Dad woke us the next day for breakfast and we clattered downstairs to the kitchen, rubbing our eyes as we went.

Mrs Carter was standing at a big, black stove very like Arthur's.

'Morning, Mrs Carter,' we said as we walked in, and she nodded.

Two land girls were already sitting at a large square table. Both had turbans tied round their heads and wore terrible overalls. *Women in trousers!* What a joke! But they both smiled and seemed very friendly.

'I'm Kitty,' said the one with dimples and curly red hair.

'And I'm Peg,' said the other, who was tubby and had wisps of dark hair poking out of her turban.

Dad introduced us and we all shook hands.

'Come and sit down,' said Kitty, tapping the chair next to her.

Mrs Carter brought us a bowl of porridge each.

'We've been here for three months,' said Kitty. 'We were drafted to help out with the farm.'

'Hard work,' said Peg. 'But we like it here, don't we, Kitty? Lovely countryside.'

'Lovely,' Kitty agreed.

'But not the cow muck,' said Freddie. 'I hate cow muck.' And the girls giggled.

'We used to live in Rochdale,' I told them. 'Our Aunt Dotty still lives there.'

'We hate her,' said Freddie.

Dad pressed his finger to his lips and said, 'Sssh!'

'So what are *you* doing here?' Peg asked Dad. 'I thought you'd be a soldier, or one of those pilots in glamorous blue uniforms flying over Germany.'

Dad looked uncomfortable.

'We're running away,' said Freddie. 'The coppers are after us.'

'Freddie,' Dad snapped. 'That's enough.' He turned and looked at Kitty. 'Sorry. He doesn't really understand.'

'I do!' said Freddie. But I took hold of his hand and tried to quieten him down.

'I don't believe in war,' Dad explained. 'My wife was killed in an air raid and I won't leave my children.'

'So you're a conchie!' said Kitty, looking across at Peg.

'Good for you,' Peg cried, and she leaned forward, lowering her voice. 'Our Gordon's in the army but I wish he wasn't. Mum didn't want him to go, but Dad said it was his duty. Now Mum worries about him all the time.'

'Well,' said Kitty, 'if it was up to me, *everybody* would refuse to fight. Where does all that fighting and killing get you? That's what I want to know.'

Mrs Carter came over to the table carrying plates of bread and dripping. 'Eat up, quick,' she said. 'You're needed in the fields. There's a lot to do at this time of year.' With that, she wiped her hands on a towel and left the kitchen.

Kitty glanced over her shoulder to make sure she had gone. 'I bet the old farmer will have you working your socks off,' she whispered. 'Just see if he don't.'

'He's always shouting at us for slacking,' said Peg, wiping her plate with her bread. 'But we don't slack, do we, Kitty?'

Kitty shook her head. 'No. We work hard. Just look at these blisters,' she said, holding out her hands. 'I'll never be a film star, will I?' And we all laughed.

'Thirty-two shillings a week, that's all we get,' Peg told us.

'Yeah,' said Kitty, glancing down at her overalls. 'Thirty-two shillings for dressing like an old man.'

They clapped their hands and hooted with laughter just as the back door opened and Mr Carter, a big, red-faced man, walked in and slammed it shut. Kitty and Peg suddenly went quiet and looked down, pretending to scrape their plates clean.

'You girls still here?' he snapped as he hung his cap on a hook. 'I've been up since five. Move yourselves.' He tugged off his wellingtons and left them by the back door. 'Get them churns to the gate before the milk lorry gets there. I'm not paying to have you sit around all day.'

Before he had even finished speaking, Kitty and Peg were on their feet and had disappeared out of the door.

The farmer walked over to the sink and turned on the tap. 'Missus!' he shouted over his shoulder as he washed his hands. 'Where's my breakfast?'

Mrs Carter came scuttling into the kitchen. Without a word, she set the frying pan on the stove and dropped in several rashers of bacon.

Mr Carter muttered under his breath as he dried his hands with a towel and wiped the mud off his face. He dropped the towel over the back of a chair and then sat down opposite Dad. He leaned forward, resting his elbows on the table. I noticed that, in spite of washing his hands, his nails were still black and he stank of cow muck. 'So you're William Butterworth, are you?'

Dad nodded.

'I understand you're a conchie.'

'Aye, I am. Not that anybody believed me back in Rochdale. I went in front of a panel but they didn't listen. They said I was making excuses and I had to fight or go to prison.'

'And the police are onto you. Is that right?'

Dad frowned and nodded. 'Aye. We were spotted.'

That horrible churning in my stomach started again and a voice in my head kept saying, *My fault we were spotted. My fault.*

Mrs Carter set a cup of tea in front of her husband and, without a word of thanks, he raised it to his lips and took a mouthful.

'So,' he said, putting the cup back on the table, 'you'd rather be on the run than go to the front with the rest of 'em, would yer?'

'I won't be parted from my kids,' Dad answered, 'and I don't believe in killing. These men in Parliament don't care how many people die. They just want power and—'

Mr Carter leaned back in his chair and waved his hand. 'Your politics are nowt to do with me, lad. My priority is keeping this farm going and I can't do that by myself with only two giggling girls to help out. I'll keep my mouth shut just as long as your work's up to scratch.'

'I'm a good worker, Mr Carter,' Dad assured him. 'And if you've got any machines that need looking at, I'm your man.'

'Mmmm,' said the farmer. 'That foreign woman who came round yesterday, she did mention you could mend things. Well, that might be useful.'

'I can work an' all,' I offered. 'I'm twelve, and I'm as strong as a lad. Honest.'

Mr Carter raised his eyebrows. 'Are you now? And what's your name?'

'Lizzie,' I said, flexing my arms and showing him my muscles.

Freddie slipped down from his chair and tapped Mr Carter on the shoulder. 'And I'm Freddie,' he said. 'I'm six and I know how to feed chickens.'

'I'm glad to hear it,' said Mr Carter, drumming his fingers on the table. 'Because you'll all have to work for your keep. I've got a harvest to bring in, with precious little help.'

Mrs Carter shuffled across the room in her slippers with a plate of bacon and eggs which she placed in front of her husband. Even though I'd had some breakfast, my mouth was watering as the food disappeared down Mr Carter's throat. Farmers ate very well, it seemed.

From then on Dad worked long hours, repairing machinery that looked as though it had come out of the ark or working in the fields when there wasn't machinery needing his attention. The days were long and hot, and the hay needed cutting and turning and baling and stacking in the barns. There was also wheat to harvest and straw to store for the winter.

Mr Carter made sure everyone worked hard. That included Freddie and me. He watched us like a hawk, and if we slacked he shouted at us, and made Freddie cry.

When he was away at market, Peg and Kitty would come over to help us.

'We'll give you a hand,' they'd say. 'And we'll have a sing-song, shall we?'

So while we worked, we sang along and we laughed a lot.

> *'I've got sixpence, jolly, jolly sixpence.*
> *I've got sixpence to last me all my life.*
> *I've got tuppence to spend and tuppence to lend*
> *And tuppence to send home to my wife.'*

It was fun when we were with Kitty and Peg but most of the time we were by ourselves. Lifting straw bales was worst. They were so heavy that we had to work together. Freddie at one side and me at the other. At the end of the day we were tired out and our arms were scratched raw and bleeding.

We only stopped work when the light faded and then we dragged ourselves back to the farmhouse. All we wanted to do was go to bed.

Freddie suffered more than I did. He was only six, and small for his age. As the weeks passed, his legs grew skinny as sticks and his little chubby face became sunken and drawn. Dad was really worried about him.

One night at the end of September, we were all in the kitchen eating our supper when Freddie slumped forward onto the table, fast asleep. Dad lifted him up and tried to wake him. 'Come on, Freddie,' he said and lifted him onto his knee. But he didn't stir.

'Give him a poke,' said Mr Carter, leaning across the table and prodding my brother with his fork. 'Wake up, lad!' he shouted.

Dad glared at the farmer. 'This isn't right and you know it,' he said. 'Too much work. He's only a child.'

'A child can work.'

'Not from morning till night. You push him too hard.'

Kitty and Peg looked at each other, eyes wide, shocked that Dad had dared to speak out like that. But Mr Carter ignored him. He didn't say a word. He just went on eating.

Dad balled his fist and thumped the table. 'Won't you listen?' When the man still didn't speak, Dad stood up with Freddie in his arms. 'Can't you see it's making him ill?'

I stood next to Dad. I wasn't going to leave him to face the old bully by himself. 'You're a hard master, Mr Carter,' I shouted.

'That's enough, Lizzie,' Dad said as he rocked Freddie backwards and forward. 'Some people are born hard.'

Mr Carter didn't seem at all bothered. He raised his fork and stuffed a piece of best steak into his mouth, chewing it slowly, then narrowing his eyes and staring at us. When he had swallowed the meat, he pointed the empty fork at Dad. 'You watch what you're saying,' he said in a low, chilling tone. 'One word from me and the police will be on you like a ton of bricks. Then what will happen to your kids, eh? Just think about that.'

Fifteen

The argument between Dad and Mr Carter changed things at the farm. From then on, Mrs Carter made sure Freddie didn't work such long hours. She showed him how to do more jobs around the farm yard – he loved looking after the chickens and collecting the eggs. When the old bully wasn't around, she put more food on our plates, too. With extra food and less work, Freddie was soon back to his old self and lively as ever.

With Mr Carter, it was different. He was even more bad-tempered, and things got worse for Dad and me. As long as it was light and there were crops to harvest, we had to work in the fields.

One day, Kitty and Peg were going to a dance at the American base not far away. We were all in the kitchen. Kitty was painting a coat of gravy browning on her legs to make it look as though she was wearing stockings.

'Oh, just wait till this war's over and I can buy the real thing,' she said. 'Won't that be a treat?'

When her legs were dry, she handed me a brown pencil. 'You've got a steady hand, Lizzie. Draw a seam up the back of my legs, will you?'

I did it very carefully because I'd never done it before, but when I'd finished Kitty was ever so pleased.

'Perfect!' she said. 'You wouldn't know I wasn't wearing stockings, would you, Peg?'

'No. You've done brilliant, Lizzie. Pity you can't come to the dance with us and have a bit of fun,' she said.

I shook my head. 'Thanks, Peg, but I'm really tired.'

'It's not fair,' said Kitty. 'The old goat works you far too hard. He doesn't give you any rest.'

Peg looked at Dad. 'Why don't you find another farm, Will? There are lots round here. Any farmer would be glad of a strong man like you.'

He shook his head. 'We're safe here,' he said. 'Things'll get better when the harvest's in.'

But things didn't get better. October passed and November grew cold. Now the fields needed ploughing and fences needed mending, hedges trimming and ditches clearing. I helped as best I could but it was mainly up to Dad. When all that was done, he was sent to the wood at the far side of the farm to clear trees. This was really hard work and I wasn't strong enough, so Dad was there by himself.

One day, halfway through the morning, Dad came staggering through the gate and into the yard. He was holding his arm – it was covered in blood.

I ran over to help him. 'What happened?' I asked, gripping his elbow and helping him into the kitchen. He sank onto a chair, his face white as bread.

Mrs Carter, who had been peeling potatoes at the sink, hurried over to look. 'Eh, William,' she said. 'That's a real nasty cut. It'll need seeing to. Lizzie, make your dad a strong cup of tea and I'll get some bandages.'

While she cleaned the wound, I made the tea and put it on the table. She had almost done and was finishing wrapping the bandage around Dad's arm when Mr Carter walked in.

'What are you doing in here, conchie?' he said.

Ever since the argument about Freddie that's what he called Dad. *Conchie*. It was a horrible word and I hated him for it. Just like I had hated Podgy Watson at school. Him and his gang, they had all used it. 'Conchie. Conchie. Conchie.'

'Having a cup of tea at my expense, are yer?' he said, walking over to Dad. The farmer placed his hands flat on the table and glared at him. 'Think you can fool my wife with a bit of a cut, eh? Well, she may be a fool but I'm not.' Then he swung his arm, sending Dad's mug of tea crashing to the floor. 'Get back to work, conchie, or you're out of here.' He looked over at his wife. 'And you, missus, get on with makin' my dinner. That's what you're here for.'

That was what he was like. He made life miserable for everybody.

Not long after that, I was working in the farmyard cleaning out the cow sheds and the pigsties when Freddie came over with some bread and cheese Mrs Carter had sent. We sat in the barn together and while we ate I got to thinking. 'We'll have to do something,' I said. 'That old bully treats Dad so bad. It's not right.'

'We could get our own back,' Freddie suggested, as he bit on the cheese.

'How do you mean?'

'Play a trick.'

Freddie was good at playing tricks.

'Have you got any ideas?' I said.

He looked at me and grinned. 'I've got a good one.'

His plan was simple. A rat-trap. We knew about traps from the builders' yard in Rochdale where Dad used to work.

'There are plenty around the barns,' said Freddie. 'Mr Carter sets them to stop the rats eating his grain.'

Mr Carter had gone to market and he wouldn't be back till late so it was a good day to put our plan into action.

'Let's do it,' I said.

We looked around the barn and found a trap buried among the hay. It was already set, waiting to snap on the neck of unsuspecting vermin. Slowly and carefully, we carried it over to the far side of the barn where Mr Carter kept a sack of special pig feed. He had a prize pig – a Gloucester Old Spot – which he kept separate from the others. He was really proud of this one and fed her the best, not just any old leftovers and potato peelings. He didn't let anyone else feed her and we had often watched him dip his hand into the pig feed to scoop some into a metal dish before taking it over to the sty.

Our plan was perfect.

I opened the top of the sack and Freddie lowered the trap carefully and buried it in the pig feed.

We knew that it would take time for something to happen, and we waited for the rest of the week but nothing did. Then, early on Saturday morning, while we were finishing our breakfast, we heard such a yelling and a commotion in the yard that we leaped up from the table and ran out to see what was going on.

'Oh, look!' said Kitty, clapping her hand over her mouth. 'It's Mr Carter.'

Across the yard by the barn, the farmer was hopping about and wailing like an animal. '*Aaaaaaaaaaaagh!*' And there, on the end of his right hand, was the rat-trap.

'Oh heavens!' said Peg. 'He's in terrible pain.' And then she turned and winked at us as if she knew we had something to do with it.

We walked towards him in no particular hurry. Kitty, who could hardly hold back her giggles, called out, 'Whatever's happened, Mr Carter? Are you hurt?'

He glared at her with wild eyes, holding out his arm in front of him. 'Am I hurt?' he yelled. 'Of course I'm hurt, you stupid girl. Can't you see it's a rat-trap? Get it off me. Somebody's put it in that sack and I want to know who.' He yelled some more and carried on jumping about the yard as if he couldn't stay still.

Kitty went up to him. 'Don't move, Mr Carter,' she said, bending over to look at the trap. 'I can't do anything if you hop like that.' The man looked up at the sky, and kept as still as he could, all the time biting his bottom lip to control the pain.

But Kitty shook her head. 'Sorry, Mr Carter. I don't know how to open it,' she said. 'Can't you do it?'

He looked back at her, his face turning purple with fury. 'Of course I can't,' he bellowed. 'Do you think I'd be standing here if I could? You,' he said, turning to Peg, 'you get it off.'

But she clapped her hands across her chest and stepped away. 'Oh no,' she said. 'I don't know how to open one of them things. I'm just a town girl. They terrify me.'

Even Dad said, 'Sorry, Mr Carter,' as the farmer leaped up and down. 'I would usually be able to open the trap but I'm all fingers and thumbs since I hurt my arm.'

Then Mrs Carter came across the yard and stood with hands on hips looking at her husband. 'It's your own fault,' she said. 'How many times have I told you to get rid of them traps? They're dangerous. Why don't you use poison like everybody else?'

This did not help the farmer's temper. His eyes bulged, and he shook with pain and anger until I thought he was going to explode. 'Just ... just get it off, woman!' he screamed. 'Look! My hand's swelling.'

His wife shrugged and said, 'I'll go and get some bandages.'

Mr Carter almost choked with rage. 'What good will bandages do, you fool? Get this thing off me!'

But she was already walking back to the farmhouse, leaving him howling and hollering.

It was then that I stepped forward. 'I think I can open the trap, Mr Carter,' I said, looking all wide-eyed and innocent. 'I'm used to setting rat-traps back home in Rochdale.'

The farmer couldn't believe that his only hope was a twelve-year-old girl. He glared at me, and his Adam's apple bobbed up and down in his throat as he swallowed nervously. 'You?' he said. 'Are you sure?'

I nodded and smiled like a little angel. 'I used to set them up and get the rats out at the builders' yard where Dad worked. Didn't I, Dad?'

And Dad nodded. 'That's right, you did.'

'Then you'd better g...get on with it,' said Mr Carter, shaking with nerves.

I took hold of the farmer's arm just under the elbow.

'Careful!' he yelled.

I looked up at him. 'I'll try my best, Mr Carter.' I gripped the end of the rat-trap in my left hand and took a lungful of air as if I was making a great effort. Then I pulled.

'Aggghhh,' he yelled. '*Aaaaagggggggg hhhhh!*'

'Oh dear,' I said. 'Did that hurt? Should we wait for Mrs Carter to come back, do you think?'

'No,' yelled the farmer. 'She's useless. Go on. Try again.'

'Are you sure?'

'Yes, yes, yes. Go on. Get it off.'

I began to fumble with the trap. Mr Carter's terrified eyes were fixed on me and sweat trickled down his forehead. I took my time, working very, very slowly. It must have seemed like for ever to the old bully.

At last the trap sprung open and everybody clapped – except the farmer who was now hugging his throbbing hand.

'Well done, Lizzie,' Kitty called. 'You deserve a treat, you do.'

97

'She certainly does,' said Mrs Carter, who had arrived carrying a bottle of Dettol and some bandages. 'I've never seen anything so well done in all my life.'

And she winked.

Sixteen

'What happened next was my fault. I should never have gone along with Freddie's trick with the rat-trap. I should never have let him do it. Just like I should never have gone to the funfair with Bernardo. It had been my fault that we'd had to leave Whiteway.

Now it was my fault again.

The farmer hated being made a fool of. He knew one of us had put the rat-trap in the sack and that we were all laughing at him behind his back. But he didn't say anything. He was too clever for that. Instead, he waited until the days were shorter and colder and he could manage without an extra worker on the farm.

One rainy afternoon in December, Freddie and I were hurrying back from collecting the eggs when we saw a black car bumping up the lane to the farmhouse.

'Police!' I said and pulled Freddie behind the pigsty. 'Go and tell Dad not to come back. He'd better hide in case they're looking for him.'

My brother didn't need telling twice. He was off, over the fence, heading for the wood where Dad was working.

From behind the wall of the sty I watched the car pull into the yard and stop. Before the policeman even had time to turn off the engine, the kitchen door opened and Mr Carter marched across the yard pulling on his coat.

'What time do you call this?' he snapped as a policeman climbed out. 'I thought you were coming yesterday? That's what you said.'

The policeman, who was much taller than Mr Carter, raised his eyebrows. 'We had an emergency, sir,' he replied as he settled his helmet on his head. 'Arresting a deserter isn't very high on my list of priorities, sir.'

Mr Carter stood in front of him. 'Oh, isn't it?' he barked. 'Well, there is a war on, you know. That man should be out there fighting. How's that for a priority?'

The driver, who was small and stocky, now stepped out and walked round the car. 'We know there's a war on, sir,' he said in a steady, unhurried voice. 'Funny you only reported this man a couple of days ago. Been working on your farm long, has he?'

That got Mr Carter flustered.

'Didn't you say he's been here a few months?'

'I... I didn't know he was on the run. He told me a pack of lies and I only found out last week.'

The tall policeman sniffed and turned his collar up against the rain. 'Right then. Let's get on with it. Where is he?'

'Follow me,' said Mr Carter and he headed towards the gate that led into the field. 'He's over there,' he said, pointing to the copse half a mile away.

I crossed my fingers, hoping that Freddie would be out of sight behind the hedgerow.

The policemen leaned on the gate, staring into the distance. 'Over there?' asked one. 'Where? I can't see him.'

'He's in that wood felling some trees.'

The policemen lifted their hands, shielding their eyes from the rain.

'You mean on the other side of that field?' said the tall one who looked at his mate and frowned. 'It's miles away.'

Mr Carter snorted. 'Don't be so soft! You'll be there in ten minutes. Go and arrest him, that's what you're here for.'

The smaller policeman shook his head. 'No point,' he said. 'He'll run away when he sees us coming. We'll get soaked, and we've no wellies.'

The tall one agreed. 'We'll ruin our uniforms with all that mud. The chief constable wouldn't like it, believe me.'

They turned and began to walk back towards the car, ignoring Mr Carter who was now spluttering with rage.

'We'll come again in the morning, sir, before your man goes out working.' They took off their helmets and climbed into the car.

The driver wound down the window and called, 'Keep him in your house until we arrive, sir. Then we can make a proper job of it.' He started up the engine and raised his hand to wave goodbye.

'Just make sure you get here tomorrow,' the farmer shouted as the car rolled away, 'or you're in serious trouble.' And, when they had disappeared down the lane, he stormed back into the house and slammed the door shut.

I stepped out from behind the pigsty and raced over the ploughed field, my feet sinking into the mud, and the icy rain stinging my face. But I didn't care. I needed to tell Dad what had happened.

By the time I reached the wood, I was gasping. I leaned against a tree until I had recovered my breath and called, 'Dad, where are you? You can come out now.'

There was a thud as Dad dropped out of a beech tree and landed at my feet. Then Freddie's face appeared through the brown leaves, which still clung to the branches. 'How do, Lizzie,' he called and grinned at me before scrambling down to Dad who waited, ready to catch him.

'Let's get out of this rain,' Dad said, 'and then you can tell me what happened.'

We followed him through the wood to a rough shelter leaning against the trunk of an old oak. Dad had made it out of birch branches and covered it in moss.

'I come here when the weather gets too bad to work,' he said, ducking through the opening.

We all squashed inside where it was dry and out of the wind and we sat on the bracken-covered floor. It was like being back in our hideout at Whiteway.

'So what did the police want?' Dad asked.

I told him what I'd overheard and how they were coming back tomorrow to arrest him.

'You did well, Lizzie,' he said. 'Now I want the pair of you to go and carry on as normal – as though you don't know what Mr Carter has planned.'

'But what are we going to do, Dad?' I asked.

'We'll have to leave,' he said, and a chill ran down my back, and I shivered at the thought of it.

'How can we leave? Mr Carter will stop us.'

'We'll go tonight when everybody's in bed.'

'Where are we going, Dad?' Freddie squealed. 'Are we going back to Whiteway? Arthur would like it and so would Lalia. And Jip.'

Dad shook his head. 'We need to get well away. We'll go to Wales,' he said. 'We'll find a farm in the mountains, miles from anywhere.'

'Just as long as we get away from that horrible man,' I said.

'I hate Mr Carter,' said Freddie. 'Hate! Hate! *Hate!*'

Dad put his arm round him. 'Now go back to the farm before they miss you,' he said. 'And don't say a word. Understood?'

Seventeen

When we walked into the farmhouse, Kitty and Peg were at the kitchen table darning socks. Mrs Carter was bending over the stove, looking in the oven.

The girls turned round and grinned. 'Well, look what the cat's dragged in!' they said, giggling and pointing at us. 'Where have you two been?'

Mrs Carter looked up. 'My goodness. You're soaked to the skin. Peg, go and get some towels so we can dry them down.' She came over and stood in front of us, shaking her head. 'What have you been up to? I thought you'd just gone to the hen house.'

I gave Freddie one of my serious looks in case he was thinking of telling the truth.

'Sorry,' I said. 'We were messing about in the field and it started to rain. We tried sheltering under the hedge but we got a bit bogged down.' It was just a small lie.

'You know, Lizzie, you should be more careful with Freddie,' she told me. 'He could get a chill from a wetting like that.'

Mrs Carter and Kitty helped us off with our soaking-wet clothes and draped them over the back of the chairs, setting them near the stove to dry. Then Peg arrived with two large towels which she wrapped round us, and she rubbed our hair until we were dizzy.

'You look like drowned rats,' Kitty said, laughing at the state of us. 'I think they need a cuppa, don't you, Mrs C?'

'Already made,' said Mrs Carter as she lifted the brown enamelled teapot. 'Sit yourselves down and have a drink. It won't be long before your meal's ready. I expect you're hungry, eh?'

Mrs Carter was very kind to us. She put mugs of tea on the table and smiled and ruffled Freddie's hair.

'It's chicken pie for tea tonight, with mashed potato then apple crumble and custard for afters. Our own cooking apples, mind. How's that then?'

It sounded wonderful.

Kitty leaned forward close to Freddie. 'If you don't want yours, little man, I'll have it,' she teased.

'No,' said Freddie. 'I'll have *yours*, Kitty. I love chicken pie. I can eat mountains of it.'

And we all laughed.

But suddenly the laughter and the chatting died when we realised that Mr Carter had walked in from the living room. 'Chicken pie?' he said, glowering at his wife. 'Good heavens, woman. Do you think I'm made of money? Who's paying for it, eh? You think you can feed your workers like royalty, do yer?' He slammed his hand on the table. 'Don't you waste my money, missus. Do you understand? No more chicken pie.'

Colour drained from Mrs Carter's face and, although she was shaking, she somehow managed to hold up her chin and look him in the eye. 'Oh, I understand, all right,' she said. 'They do the work and you get the food. You're a cruel master, Jacob Carter, and I don't know why I've put up with you all these years.'

The blow came without warning, swiping across her face and sending her reeling backwards, crashing into the stove.

Freddie squealed. Kitty and Peg stood up and screamed, 'Mr Carter! No!'

But he turned and pointed at them with a threatening finger. 'Stay out of this, you two, or you'll get some of the same.'

And they slumped back onto their chairs, their mouths hanging open.

Mrs Carter, with her hand on her cheek, ran out of the room sobbing. No one dared go after her. The old bully stood in the middle of the kitchen, glowering at us until he snorted and stormed towards the back door.

'You'll find me in The King's Head,' he barked. 'My own home is full of fools.'

He snatched his coat off the hook and disappeared into the yard.

When he had gone, Freddie burst into tears and Kitty hugged him. 'Don't you worry, Freddie,' she said, giving him a squeeze. 'He's just a mean old man.'

Freddie looked up at her. 'I h-hate him,' he stuttered as the tears poured down his cheeks. 'I'm g-glad we're going away—'

'No, Freddie,' I said in an attempt to stop him talking, but it was too late.

'We won't see him no more, Dad promised. Mr Carter's a horrible man. We're going tonight and we'll find somewhere nice to live. In Wales. Dad said so.'

Once Freddie got started, there was no stopping him. Peg and Kitty sat and listened, their eyes wide with surprise as he told them about the police coming to the farm.

Peg turned and looked at me. 'Is that right?' she asked. 'Are you leaving tonight?' I nodded. There was no point in denying it now. She leaned back in her chair. 'How will you get away without the old goat seeing you?'

'Dunno,' I said. 'But we've got to go tonight or they'll take Dad to prison in the morning.'

'Well,' she said, looking at Kitty, 'we'll help you all we can, won't we?'

'We will,' Kitty agreed. 'I've got some savings upstairs. You can have 'em.'

'Mine too,' said Peg. 'Your dad will need money to look after you two. It might be a while before he gets work again.'

Kitty stood up. 'You must promise me this,' she said. 'You mustn't tell your dad about the money until you're well away from here.'

'Why?' Freddie asked.

I knew. But then I was older.

'He probably won't take it, you see,' Peg explained. 'Not from a couple of silly land girls, anyway.' Then she winked and laughed. 'So you're in charge.'

I tried to protest. After all, Kitty and Peg didn't earn much. But they insisted on giving us money. I knew it would help – so in the end, I agreed.

Kitty ran up to her bedroom and when she came back she was carrying two small cloth bags. 'Here's the dosh,' she said, and I heard the chink of coins and the rustle of pound notes when she put them on the table.

'Peg,' said Kitty. 'Bring me their coats, will you? I've got an idea where we can hide that lot.'

She picked a pair of scissors from the sewing box.

'I'm going to slit the lining,' she said. 'The bag of money can go inside and then I'll stitch it up again, see. I don't suppose anyone will notice.'

'Good idea,' said Peg, putting the coats on the table. 'Pass me the scissors and I'll do this one.'

I stood behind them and watched. 'That's really clever. We'll be like smugglers.'

'Or burglars,' said Freddie, jumping up and down. 'Or thieves or—'

Then Dad walked in.

Eighteen

'I'm back,' Dad called as he pulled off his boots by the door. 'By heck, it's cold out there,' he said, clapping his hands together and blowing on his fingers.

The money was right there on the table. So were our coats with the linings slit open.

Dad had hardly got his own coat off when Freddie raced across the room and flung his arms around Dad's waist. 'Guess what?'

I thought Freddie was going to tell him about the money. But he didn't.

'It's Mr Carter,' said my brother. 'He's been horrible. He hit Mrs Carter ever so hard. Honest, he did! He made her cry.'

Dad looked across at Peg and Kitty who nodded sheepishly as if to say, *Yes, that's right. He did hit her.* Nobody spoke for a while.

It was Kitty who broke the silence. 'Guess what we're having for tea, William?' she said, tapping her nose. 'Can't you smell it? It's chicken pie.'

'With mashed potatoes,' Freddie added.

'Well, then,' said Dad. 'Let me get to the sink and clean this mud off. I can't sit and eat with you all if I'm looking like a tramp, can I?'

As he walked past the table, I squeezed my eyes shut

hoping he wouldn't spot the money and the coats. When I opened them again, he was leaning on the back of a chair looking across at Peg and Kitty.

'You two ladies look busy,' he said. 'What are you doing?'

Peg smiled at Dad, calm as you like. 'Just a bit of repair work,' she said as she threaded cotton into a needle.

I looked at the table. Mrs Carter's sewing box was there. But the money had gone and the coats were draped over Peg and Kitty's knees.

'I don't know what your little scallywags get up to,' said Kitty, 'but their coats have holes that are letting the cold in.'

Dad laughed, walked over to the sink and turned on the tap. 'You two girls are real good sorts,' he said. 'I'm terrible at sewing. Thanks for doing that.'

He cupped his hands under the running water and splashed it over his face before rubbing off the mud that had caked his cheeks, his neck and even his ears. Then he took the bar of soap and repeated the process all over again.

While he was at the sink, Peg and Kitty winked at us, snatched the little bags of money off their laps where they had hidden them, and stuffed them into the lining of our coats. By the time Dad had dried himself off with a towel, they were quietly stitching up the holes again.

'There's tea in the pot, William,' said Peg. 'I expect you'll be ready for that.'

'Right,' said Dad as he hung the towel on a rail. 'Working in them woods is thirsty work. It's cold work an' all.'

He poured himself a mug of tea and sat at the table and

we listened while he told us what he'd seen in the wood that day. He was telling us about a new badger sett on the edge of the wood when Mrs Carter walked into the kitchen. She looked terrible. Her left cheek was purple and swollen, and her eyes were puffed up from crying. When Dad saw the bruises on her face, his mouth fell open. She must have known how bad she appeared but she still looked Dad straight in the eye. 'William, I'd like a word,' she said in a quivery sort of voice. 'Peg, Kitty, take the children into the front room, please.'

Kitty hesitated.

'Now. Thank you,' she insisted.

The girls stood up and bundled us through the door. Mrs Carter closed it behind us.

Kitty took Freddie's hand and led him down the hall to the living room. But I didn't want to leave.

'No!' I said, pushing Peg away. 'I've got to know what's going on.'

'Sssh!' said Peg. 'She'll hear you.'

'But why does she want to talk to Dad?'

She shook her head and shrugged.

'I need to know what's happening, Peg. If I can't be in the kitchen, I can listen, can't I?'

Peg took hold of my hand and tugged me away. 'No, Lizzie. You shouldn't go eavesdropping on private conversations.'

'But Dad might be in trouble.'

Before she knew it, I had slipped out of her grasp and was

back at the kitchen door with my ear pressed to the keyhole, listening.

I heard the scraping of the chairs on the quarry-tiled floor as Dad and Mrs Carter sat at the table.

'Is something wrong, Mrs Carter?' asked Dad. 'You don't look at all well. Shouldn't you go and have a lie down?'

'I'm well enough, William,' she said in a quiet voice. 'Thank you for asking.'

'Then what did you want to talk to me about? Have the children been misbehaving?'

When Mrs Carter spoke next, her voice was stronger. 'No, they haven't. They're grand.'

'Then what?'

There was a pause.

'I'm not a disloyal woman, William. You must understand that,' she said, hesitating as if it was hard for her to speak. 'But my husband can be a very difficult man...' There was another pause. Much longer this time.

Then Dad spoke in a low voice. 'Yes, he can be, but Mr Carter took us in when we needed help. I'm grateful for that.'

'He's given you no wages, William,' Mrs Carter snapped back, her voice trembling. 'So you've nothing to thank him for. You're a hard worker and he's kept you as long as you were useful to him. That's all.'

'Well, I...'

'Listen, William. I have to tell you something shocking.'

'What?'

'I never thought I'd be saying this. I can't believe it myself.'

Dad didn't reply.

'My husband,' she continued in a shaky voice, 'my husband has sent for the police and they're coming here early tomorrow morning to arrest you.'

I gasped when I heard her say that. So she knew about the police and she was on our side! That swipe from Mr Carter must have been the last straw.

'You have to leave tonight,' she said. 'I'll help you. I'll make sure that my husband sleeps like a log. He'll not hear you go. And I'll put out some food for you to take and I'll get some of my husband's old clothes. You'll need extra in this weather.'

'I don't know what to say,' said Dad.

'Say nothing,' Mrs Carter answered. 'You get yourself away from here tonight.'

But her next words struck me like a hammer blow.

'Leave the children here,' she said. 'I've grown very fond of them, you know, and I'll look after them – you can be sure of that. They'll come to no harm with me.'

I couldn't stop myself. I burst through the door into the kitchen. 'No!' I yelled at Mrs Carter and flung myself at Dad, 'He's not going by himself. We're going with him.' And I clung to him like a limpet.

Slowly Dad peeled my fingers from round his neck, gripped my arms and looked me right in the eye. 'Listen to me, Lizzie. There's no way I'm leaving you behind. Isn't that what we said right at the beginning?' He turned back to Mrs Carter. 'Thank you. I'm grateful,' he said. 'But our family sticks together, come what may.'

113

She nodded. 'I understand.' I thought she looked a little bit sad. 'But don't let my husband guess what you're up to. Not a word. Not a hint. Go to bed at the usual time and wait until midnight before you come down. I'll make sure he's sound asleep by then.'

'We'll be ever so quiet, Mrs Carter,' I promised, and she smiled at me and reached out, putting her hand on my cheek.

'You're a good girl, Lizzie,' she said before turning back to Dad. 'Head towards Eastcombe. You know where that is, don't you?'

Dad nodded.

'There's a farm on the outskirts with big barns where you can shelter for the night – but mind you get well away in the morning once it's light. The police will come looking for you when they find you've gone.'

She pushed her chair away from the table and stood up. 'Anyway,' she said, smoothing her pinny. 'Enough of this. I've got a chicken pie that's ready to be eaten. It's time we all had our tea.'

She walked briskly to the door and called down the hall for the others to come back. Then she went over to the stove and took out the biggest pie I'd seen for ages. If this was our last meal at the farmhouse, it was going to be a good one.

Nineteen

Mr Carter didn't come home from the pub in time for tea and Peg reckoned he'd be back later with a sore head.

The chicken pie was perfect — covered in a crispy crust and swimming in gravy, with potatoes and carrots as well. We ate until we were full to bursting. Afterwards, we lit the oil lamps and drew the curtains and got out the playing cards. We were sitting round the table in the middle of the second game when Freddie started one of his coughs. It was nothing really but they all made a fuss of him.

'You got soaking wet this afternoon, didn't you, Freddie?' said Kitty, and he nodded.

Mrs Carter frowned and put her hand on his forehead. 'He's hot,' she said, looking across at Dad. 'I'll get something for his chest. Then you'd best get him up to bed.'

Freddie's mouth drooped. 'I'm not going on my own,' he said, his eyes brimming with tears. 'You've got to come too, Lizzie.' And he burst out sobbing and wailing just as the back door opened and Mr Carter staggered in.

'What's that child blathering about?' he barked. 'Can't I have a bit of peace and quiet in my own house? Shut him up, will yer?'

Dad cradled Freddie in his arms. 'Shush now, son,' he said. 'Don't cry.'

'You make too much fuss of your young-uns,' the old bully sneered as he took off his coat and dropped it on the floor. 'Where's my supper, missus? Why isn't it ready, eh?'

He staggered across the kitchen, bumping against the sideboard and finally flopping into his chair. He picked up his knife and fork and banged them impatiently on the table until a plate of chicken pie and mash was put in front of him.

Freddie, terrified of Mr Carter, had stopped crying but was suddenly overcome with a fit of coughing. The farmer pointed his fork at Dad. 'I told you to shut that lad up.' Which made Freddie cry again.

'I'll take him to bed,' Dad said.

'Aye, you'd better,' said the farmer, not bothering to turn round. 'Good riddance.'

'And good riddance to you!' said Freddie with tears trickling down his cheeks. 'I hate you.'

Everybody in the room held their breath, terrified that Freddie might say something about us leaving. But he was caught by another bout of coughing and Dad hurried towards the door. I followed.

'Wait a minute,' said Mrs Carter, taking a jar out of the cupboard. 'Here. Rub this on his chest, William. It'll do him the world of good.' And she handed Dad a pot of goose grease.

Mr Carter looked up at his wife and, with his mouth full of pie, he made a grumbling noise – but she took no notice.

We walked out of the kitchen and Peg and Kitty called, 'Night, night. Sleep tight. Don't let the bedbugs bite,' as they always did. I felt really sad that we couldn't say goodbye properly.

I hated the smell of goose grease. It made me feel sick.

'Never mind the smell,' said Dad when we were up in the bedroom. 'It'll help Freddie's cough. We don't want him to get ill, do we? That goose grease and a nice warm bed will have him right as rain by the time we leave.' And he rubbed it into Freddie's chest and across his back.

We didn't get undressed that night. Dad told us to just take off our shoes and climb into bed.

'Another adventure, Freddie,' he said, sitting on the edge of the bed, stroking my brother's head. 'We'll have fun, eh?'

Freddie, who had stopped crying by then, nodded and snuggled down under the blankets, coughing for a while before he fell asleep. I helped Dad pack. He said we had to travel light and we should only take one case. That meant leaving some things behind – but we planned to wear a double layer of clothes to keep out the cold.

'We'd better get some sleep, Lizzie,' Dad said and he put the suitcase by the bedroom door with our gas mask boxes on top, ready for the morning.

I lay in bed wondering where we'd be this time tomorrow. I suppose I must have slept, because the next thing I heard was a tapping on the bedroom door and the creak of the hinges as it opened.

I sat up and rubbed my eyes and then reached for my glasses. Mrs Carter was standing in the doorway, holding a candle and Dad was already up, pulling on his jumper.

'Are you all awake?' she whispered.

Dad nodded. 'Freddie's still asleep but I'll get him up now.'

'Come down to the kitchen as soon as you're ready.' she said. 'And don't worry about my husband. I gave him an extra-large glass of whiskey before he went to bed. He's snoring fit to wake the dead.' Then she left, closing the door behind her.

It was hard to wake Freddie, so Dad carried him downstairs and gave him a drink of water. When he finally opened his eyes, Dad fetched his coat off the hook and put it on him.

Mrs Carter had parcelled up some sandwiches and bread and cheese as she had promised. Dad stuffed them into his coat pockets and thanked her.

'I want you to promise me you'll take care of these children, William,' she said.

Dad smiled and took her hand. 'I'll look after them all right and I'll see that we stay together.'

'Good man,' she said, and I saw her wipe away a tear.

Freddie, sitting at the table, had fallen asleep again so Dad picked him up and carried him over his shoulder to the door. When I opened it, I felt the full blast of the bitter winter wind on my face.

'Good luck to you all,' called Mrs Carter softly as we walked with our heads down, into the cold, black night.

Crossing the ploughed fields made the muscles of my legs ache but I was glad I was wearing wellies. If they didn't keep my feet warm, at least they kept them dry.

'Are we going to that farm in Eastcombe, Dad?'

'I don't think I can carry Freddie that far,' he said. 'We'll have to spend the night in the wood.'

'In the shelter?'

'Aye,' he said. 'Will that do, Lizzie? It'll keep us dry and warm for a few hours until it gets light. Then we'll have to be off again.'

We plodded on, bent against the driving wind, and now and then, when the moon came out from behind the clouds, the ground sparkled white with frost and I could see the wood in the distance.

I glanced at the stars in the black velvet sky. 'Not far now, Mum,' I whispered to the brightest star. 'We'll be all right, won't we?'

Twenty

Once we reached the wood, the trees blocked out any light that came from the moon. When I felt the needle-fine thorns dig into my legs, I knew I'd walked into a patch of brambles. I tried to pull myself free, but the more I struggled, the more tangled I became until I toppled over and fell onto the soaking ground.

'Dad, I can't get up!' I yelled. Dad set Freddie on the ground and he came hurrying back to where I was lying and cut me free with his pocket knife.

'Thanks,' I said, rubbing my scratched and bleeding knees before I got up again and limped after him.

The shelter was on the far side of the wood and once I'd squeezed in through the small opening I flopped onto the soft bed of bracken. It was a tight squeeze for the three of us but we soon snuggled down, glad to be out of the wind. Dad took off his coat and spread it over us all like a heavy blanket. Together we were warm as toast.

All the way from the farm to the wood Freddie had slept on Dad's shoulder, but now that he was lying down, he was restless, tossing and turning and coughing every few minutes.

'I wish he'd shut up, Dad. Can't you stop him?'

'Try to ignore it and get some sleep, Lizzie. We've got a

long walk tomorrow.' He talked on but his voice faded as my eyelids grew heavy and the sweet smell of the bracken soon sent me into a deep, deep sleep.

The next morning, Dad shook me awake. 'Get up, Lizzie,' he said. 'We've got to go.'

I opened my eyes quickly and I was surprised to see a bright light creeping through the roof of the shelter. I poked my head out of the opening and saw that the wood was now carpeted in a thick layer of white.

I wriggled back inside. 'It's snowing,' I said.

Freddie must have heard me. He opened his eyes and sat up, looking more like his old self. 'Snow!' he squealed with excitement. 'Can we make a snowman? Can we, Dad?'

'We need to get moving,' Dad told him. 'This snow won't make walking any easier for us and the police could arrive at the farm any time.'

Freddie started to protest until he was overtaken by a fit of coughing and I had to rub his back until it stopped.

'We'll have some breakfast before we set off, eh?' Dad said and gave us one of the sandwiches Mrs Carter had made for us. They were as thick as doorsteps, with pieces of chicken between slices of home-made bread. As I bit into mine, I thought of last night's chicken pie and I closed my eyes remembering how it tasted. Magic!

We ate our feast without a word, soon feeling stronger and warmer for it. Then Dad said, 'Right. We'd better be off. We'll be walking for a long time today.'

I buttoned up my coat, which was still wet from the fall in the wood, and wrapped my scarf twice around my neck for good measure.

'I'll carry the suitcase, Lizzie. You did a grand job last night. I know it's heavy.'

We stepped out of the shelter and into the falling snow. Dad went first and I walked behind him, keeping my eyes fixed on the ground, on the lookout for tree roots and brambles.

'Walk behind me, Freddie,' I said, pushing him out of the way.

'Why do I have to?'

'Because you're smaller.'

'What's that got to do with it?'

'You might fall over.'

'Why?'

'Brambles will trip you up.'

'Why?'

'Oh, because!'

Once out of the wood, we set off across the fields. The snow was falling steadily but slowly at first, settling layer on layer. But later, it grew heavier and the flakes were gigantic, drifting down, covering our shoulders and our chests, and sticking to our gloves so that we looked like walking snowmen.

Then things got worse. The wind suddenly picked up and turned the snowfall into a blinding blizzard. One minute it swirled around us like a white fog, the next, it drove at us with a million icy darts stabbing at our faces. It was impossible to see where we were going. We leaned forward into the wind, gasping for breath.

'Can we stop, Dad?' Freddie shouted over the noise of the blizzard. 'I'm tired.'

Dad looked at him. 'No, son, we can't. But I'll give you a piggyback, eh?' Dad hoisted him onto his back, I picked up the case and we carried on as best we could, one slow step at a time.

Walking behind Dad meant I was sheltered from the worst of the wind, and stepping into his footsteps made it easier for me.

I tapped him on his shoulder. 'Dad!' I yelled above the wind. 'Won't the police see our footprints? Won't they follow us?'

Dad turned. 'Don't worry, Lizzie. The snow is falling so thick it's covering them up.' This made me feel better. But some time later, halfway up a steeply sloping bank, he suddenly stopped and stood shielding his eyes with his hand and looked first one way and then the other.

'What's up?' I asked him.

'It's this snow, Lizzie. Everything looks the same,' he said. 'I'm not sure where we are. I'm not even sure we're going in the right direction.'

'I'll go to the top, Dad,' I said, pointing to the brow of the hill. 'I might be able to see something from up there.'

I put the case down and trudged on ahead, but when I reached the highest point the snow was falling so densely it was like a great white curtain, blocking everything out.

I cleared the snowflakes from my glasses and stared again into the distance, not wanting to give up. Then, out of the snowy mist, I saw an outline of something. I waited with my eyes fixed on the spot to make sure it was really there. It was. Definitely.

I hurried back, leaping and jumping in my excitement. Sometimes I slid. Sometimes I rolled down the hill until I reached Dad and Freddie who were crouching under a hedge sheltering from the snow.

'Did you see anything, Lizzie?' Dad asked.

I brushed the snow off my coat and squatted beside them, gasping for breath. 'I ... did,' I panted.

'What was it?'

'A church spire.'

'If there's a church,' said Dad, 'there must be a village nearby. That means we'll find somewhere to shelter until this snow stops.' He looked down at us and smiled. 'Come on, then. Not far now.'

Twenty-One

All the time we walked, we fixed our eyes on that church spire. At first it was a misty form in the distance but as we walked on through the snow it became clearer, and beyond it we could see houses – high ones, low ones, higgledy-piggledy all squashed together.

'We can't get too near to the village,' I explained to Freddie.

'Why not?' he asked.

'Cos we don't want to be seen, do we?'

'We need a barn,' said Dad, 'so we can shelter from the snow. We'll have to carry on to Wales tomorrow.'

Freddie's face fell. 'Not more walking!'

'Sorry, son,' Dad said, patting his head. 'One more day, I promise. Then we'll be well away.'

We trudged on, getting nearer to the village, when I spotted something across the fields. 'Look, Dad, over there!' I said, pointing to a low wooden building with a clock on the top. 'It's perfect.'

Dad looked. 'That's a cricket pavilion. Well spotted, Lizzie. That will do just fine. Come on.'

We raced ahead with a sudden burst of energy and when we reached the building Dad dropped the case on the ground while we searched for a way in.

Round the back, Dad pointed to a tiny window that had been left open. 'Do you think you could squeeze through there, son?'

My brother grinned and nodded. 'Course I can,' he said. Dad bent over so that he could climb onto his back and reach up to the window.

Freddie managed to push his head and shoulders through the opening. 'I'm all right now,' he shouted, wriggling bit by bit through the window until he disappeared. Then we heard a thud as he fell and he must have landed in a heap on the floor. '*OOOOWWWW!*' he yelled. 'That hurt!'

'You all right?' Dad called.

'My knee's bleeding.'

'Could you unlock the door and let us in?' Dad asked.

'I'm just rubbing my knee, and then I will.'

'Well, get a move on!' I shouted – which was a bit mean, but I was freezing.

We raced round to the door at the front

Freddie was ages fiddling with the lock. I don't know what was so difficult. I was standing ankle-deep in snow and my feet had already turned to blocks of ice.

Then the door finally opened and Freddie shouted, 'I did it,' and we rushed in out of the cold.

Not that it was warm inside. It wasn't. The roof had a few holes in it and snow had found its way in and settled in small heaps on the wooden floor. But it didn't matter. It was better than being outside.

'Right,' said Dad. 'First things first. We'll take our wet

clothes off and hope they dry before tomorrow. Get some dry things out of the suitcase.'

So we stripped off our coats and jumpers – right down to our vests. Standing there in next to nothing, my teeth were chattering like marbles in a bag. We put on as many dry layers as we could – but somehow couldn't get warm.

'What about those things over there,' I said, pointing to some white cricket jumpers hanging on a row of hooks. 'We could wear those.'

There were twenty or more and I took one off a hook and pulled it over my head. It was enormous. My hands disappeared inside the sleeves and the jumper dropped well past my knees. 'This is as warm as crumpets,' I told them. Then I took a second one and made a cushion out of it and sat with my arms wrapped around my knees.

Freddie put one on too and that covered him from head to toe. 'It's very scratchy,' he said.

'It's warm, isn't it?'

'Yes.'

'Which is best?' I asked. 'Scratchy or cold?'

He decided to keep it on, and when he started coughing again, Dad wrapped another one round his shoulders.

We made a sort of mattress out of the rest of the jumpers, and by the time we had done that the light had started to fade. Dad pulled out what was left of Mrs Carter's sandwiches and we drank water from the sink in the corner, but it was so icy that I could feel it drop into my stomach and settle like an ice cube.

The room was soon dark as pitch. We hadn't candles or anything, so there was nothing to do but go to sleep. We snuggled together on the heap of jumpers and put even more on top of us like blankets.

But I couldn't sleep. For one thing, flakes of snow drifted through gaps in the roof and landed on my nose – I was sure it had turned blue with cold. Then there was the rattling of the windows as the wind whipped round the cricket pavilion, howling and moaning all through the night. On top of that, there was Freddie's coughing. So I didn't sleep.

Not that I minded. I lay there, looking through the clear glass of the window, gazing at the sky which was heavy with snow clouds. But Mum's star was there. The only one. 'Thanks for finding us this place,' I whispered. 'It's very nice, but could you please get us to Wales as quick as you can?'

Twenty-Two

I must have fallen asleep for a while because when I opened my eyes the room was filled with daylight. Dad was kneeling by Freddie, wiping his forehead with a handkerchief.

I pushed away the heap of jumpers and sat up. 'What's wrong?' I asked.

'Freddie's really poorly,' said Dad, sighing a deep sigh. 'And to make matters worse, it's snowing again.'

I went over to the window and stood on tiptoe to look out. The snow was even deeper than yesterday. It was almost knee-high and falling in big fat flakes. It didn't look as though it was going to stop. The wind was howling across the fields, sending it into deep drifts against the hedges.

'It must have been snowing all night,' said Dad. 'I don't know what we're going to do.'

'A bit of snow won't stop us. We'll manage.'

Dad rubbed his hand across his mouth and shook his head. 'I don't think so, Lizzie.'

'Yes. We'll be like Scott of the Antarctic!' I insisted. 'There was loads of snow when he went exploring.'

Dad came over to the window, gripped my shoulders and looked me straight in the eye. 'Listen. It's not just you and me, Lizzie. Freddie won't be able to walk in this, he's too small and he's not well. He's been coughing all night.'

I went over to check. 'I think he's OK, Dad. He's just tired. Give him another half an hour and he'll be wide awake.'

Dad didn't reply. He kneeled down by Freddie's side, placing a hand on his forehead and then on his cheeks. Freddie stirred, tossing his head from side to side, but he didn't open his eyes.

'He's got a temperature,' Dad explained. 'He's too ill to go out in this weather, Lizzie.' Then he tucked the jumpers round Freddie's chin and stood up.

We waited all morning, sitting by him, hoping he would get better. Once, when Dad wasn't looking, I shook his shoulder – but he still didn't wake up. And when Dad tried spooning water into his mouth, it only made him cough more than ever.

Later on, the snow finally stopped, the sun shone in through the dusty windows and the icicles on the roof began to melt.

'I've made a decision, Lizzie,' said Dad. 'We've got to get help.'

'But you said we had to hide.'

He sighed and looked away. 'Your brother's ill,' he said. '*Very* ill.'

'But he'll get better.'

Dad shook his head. 'Freddie needs medicine. We can't stay here, Lizzie. We've no fire and we've hardly any food left.' He walked over to the window and pressed his head against the glass. 'I've been selfish. I know that now and I can't put Freddie's life at risk.'

'But, Dad...'

'No, Lizzie,' he said, turning to face me. 'Collect your things and put on your boots. Two pairs of socks, mind.' He walked over to Freddie and kneeled by his side again. 'We'll go now and find a doctor.'

Dad wrapped Freddie in the biggest cricket jumper for extra warmth. But when he lifted him off the bed, Freddie flopped like a rag doll, his cheeks flushed scarlet. Dad carried him, while I walked behind in his footsteps, with the case in one hand and the gas masks over my shoulder.

There were houses at the bottom of the hill and we slithered in the soft snow trying our best to keep our footing. The nearest cottage was on the edge of the village. Smoke was rising from its chimney so I knew that someone was in.

'That'll do,' said Dad, nodding towards it.

'I'll see if somebody can help us,' I said, and I strode ahead through the deep drifts of snow, not caring when it spilled over my wellies and melted down my legs. Someone had cleared the path to the cottage and I raced up and banged hard on the door until it opened.

'Please can you help us?' I gasped as an old man stood peering at me through silver-rimmed glasses.

But he said nothing. He just stared.

'My little brother's ill,' I said, and I turned and pointed to Dad who wasn't far behind me, with Freddie in his arms.

'Well, I'm blowed,' said the old man at last. 'Whatever's the matter?'

Before I could answer, a lady appeared behind him and looked out at us over her husband's shoulder. 'Oh dear,' she said, covering her mouth with her fingers. 'Whatever's the matter, child?'

'Indeed,' the old man nodded. 'That's just what I said.'

Dad was now standing behind me. 'I'm sorry to bother you but my little boy is ill and...'

The lady gave her husband a nudge. 'Let them come in, Jeremiah. It's bitterly cold out there. Come in. Come in.'

They took us into a small room with a log fire burning in the grate.

'Put your boy on the settee,' said the lady, pushing her white hair back from her face. 'Take your wet things off, you must be frozen. Jeremiah, get a blanket from upstairs while I make some tea.'

The old couple disappeared while Dad settled Freddie on the settee. I left my coat and boots in the hall and sat on the hearth rug close to the fire, feeling the warmth creeping through my bones. But Freddie was coughing again.

'I need to get my boy to a doctor,' said Dad when the man returned with the blankets. 'Is there one in the village?'

The old man looked puzzled. 'A doctor you say?'

'Yes.'

The old lady, who was called Mrs Bazley, arrived with a tray of tea. 'The doctor lives on the high street,' she said. 'He's not far away but you mustn't go.'

'But my boy is really ill.'

'And I can see that you're worn out too.' She turned to her husband. 'Put your coat on, Jeremiah. Go and fetch Doctor Mackenzie. Tell him we've got a wee one here who's very poorly.' Then she looked at Dad and smiled. 'Don't you worry. The doctor's a good man. He'll come.'

I don't know whether it was the tea or the blazing fire – but I suddenly felt safe and happy. If the old couple would let us stay for a few days until the snow melted and Freddie was better, then everything would be all right. We could carry on to Wales.

Twenty-Three

Dr Mackenzie arrived in less than half an hour. He banged the snow off his shoes at the door and marched into the small front room. He was older than Dad, with deep-set eyes, huge bushy eyebrows and furrow lines that ran between them.

'Well, well, well,' he said. 'What have we here?' He tossed his coat over a chair and went across to Freddie, still lying on the settee, covered in a blanket.

'Mmmm,' he said, bending over and resting his hand on Freddie's forehead. 'How long has he been like this?'

'He's had a cough for a day or two,' Dad replied. 'But he got worse last night.'

The doctor opened a large black leather bag, pulled out a stethoscope and pressed it against Freddie's chest.

'He gets loads of coughs,' I said. 'Especially in winter. Dad rubs him with goose grease and he always gets better.'

Dr Mackenzie looked up at me and smiled. 'And where were you living before you came to see Mr and Mrs Bazley?'

I wasn't sure what to say, so I didn't say anything.

Dad looked really sad. The corner of his mouth twitched nervously and he sighed and shook his head. 'We were on our way to Wales when the snow came. So we spent the night in the cricket pavilion. It was very cold. Freddie already had a bad chest but he got really sick in the night.'

Dr Mackenzie stood up and straightened his back. 'So you came knocking on Mr Bazley's door, eh?'

He nodded.

The doctor folded his stethoscope into the bag and looked at Dad. 'I'd say you were a fit young man. Explain to me why you aren't fighting for your country? Haven't you been called up?'

Dad didn't answer. Instead he sank onto a chair and held his head in his hands.

I sat by him and snuggled into him. 'It's not his fault,' I said to the doctor. 'It's all because of this horrible war. None of this would have happened but for Adolf Hitler. I hate him. He's ruined everything.'

'Sssh, Lizzie,' said Dad, patting my hand.

'Then I take it you are on the run,' Doctor Mackenzie said, snapping the bag shut.

Dad raised his head and looked up at him. 'I'm a conscientious objector,' he said in a low voice.

'Then what are you doing on the run? You could be doing war work, couldn't you?'

'I went to the tribunal but they turned me down,' Dad said. 'They told me I had to join up or go to prison.' Dad's face suddenly flushed pink. 'I don't agree with the war, doctor. I won't fight. I won't kill. I only want what's best for my family.'

The doctor put his hand on Dad's shoulder. 'Your son is very sick,' he said. 'Is that what's best for your family?'

Dad covered his eyes and shook his head from side to side. 'I don't know what's best anymore,' he said. 'Whatever I do seems wrong.'

The doctor stood still, rubbing his hand across his chin. 'I can give your son some medicine.'

Dad looked up. 'I'm sorry, doctor. I've no money to pay you.'

'No matter,' he said. 'I can see that things are hard. But it will be a few days before your little boy is well. He mustn't go out until he's strong again.'

'They can stay here,' said Mr Bazley. 'We'll look after the boy.'

'I'm sure you will, Jeremiah,' said the doctor, smiling at the old man. Then he turned to Dad. 'But what about you? How much longer can you go on putting your children at risk like this?'

Dad looked up at him, his eyes lifeless as if he knew what was coming.

'I'm afraid I will have to report you to the police,' Dr Mackenzie informed him. 'It's my duty.'

'No!' I said, jumping up and grabbing hold of the doctor's sleeve. 'You mustn't do that. They'll take Dad and put him in prison. No! Don't! Please!'

Dad pulled me away and held me while I blubbed like a baby. I couldn't stop – I couldn't bear the thought of Dad leaving us.

Dr Mackenzie took a bottle of medicine from his bag and gave it to Mrs Bazley. 'One teaspoonful three times a day,' he said, reaching for his coat. 'Give him plenty to drink and some good soup if you've got some.'

'I'll see he gets it, doctor,' she said. 'I'll take care of him.'

'You're a kind woman, Florence,' said the doctor, pulling on his coat. 'I'll come back tomorrow to see how he is.'

'Very well,' Mrs Bazley nodded. 'But perhaps it would be best if you waited until morning before telephoning the police. The snow's deep and they won't thank you for getting them out on a day like this.'

He sighed. 'Maybe you're right, Florence. Maybe you're right.' Then he opened the door and walked away down the road to the village.

By that evening, Freddie wasn't coughing so much. His face was still pale and washed out but he was sitting up drinking soup that Mrs Bazley had made specially, with bread to dip in it.

'He'll be back to normal tomorrow, Dad,' I said. 'I bet he'll be strong enough to get to Wales, don't you? With that medicine an' all. If we leave early, we can get away before the police get here, eh?'

Dad's shoulders slumped as if they had the worries of the world sitting on them. He took my hand and pulled me close. 'I need to talk to you, Lizzie,' he said, and my stomach clamped tight.

'No, Dad,' I said, my voice shaking with fear. 'There's nothing to talk about. We're going to Wales just like we planned and you're going to get a job and we'll all be together.'

'Lizzie, I...'

'No, don't say it, Dad.' I held my hand across his mouth to stop him speaking.

But he prised it away and wrapped his arms tight round me. 'Listen,' he said softly. 'I'm sorry, Lizzie. We're not going to Wales. No more running away. I can't put you through it.

Look at what has happened to Freddie. Another night on the run and he might have died.'

'No,' I said, beating my fists against his chest. 'We've got to go.'

But Dad held me tighter and whispered in my ear. 'I need you to look after your brother, Lizzie. Will you promise me that? Will you? Please?'

Tears were streaming down my face, and my throat was so tight that I couldn't speak. I buried my face in his chest and felt his cheek rest against my hair.

'That promise is important, Lizzie,' he said, 'because when the police come tomorrow morning, I'm going to give myself up.'

Twenty-Four

They came for Dad the next morning. I don't remember much about it except that I shouted and bawled and clung onto him until a policeman dragged me away and kept hold of me while another one pushed Dad into the car. And as they drove away, I remember banging my fists on the back window and screaming, 'Dad! Dad!' over and over.

Mrs Bazley hurried after me through the snow, still wearing her old slippers. She wrapped her arms round me and tried to calm me down. She kept saying, 'Now, now, my lovely,' but I shook her away and I couldn't stop the tears. Even when she'd taken me back to the house, I still cried. I cried all day until I had no tears left, then I curled up and refused to speak to anybody.

Freddie, who was still feeling poorly, sat on Mr Bazley's knee, his eyes swollen with crying, sucking his thumb. Mr Bazley tried to cheer him up by saying nursery rhymes, but he was so old that he had forgotten most of them.

We didn't know where our dad was being taken and we didn't know what would happen to us next. Not that we cared about ourselves. As far as we were concerned, our world had ended. Dad was gone. We were no longer a family.

*

That night, the sky darkened and the stars came out, I looked out of the window for Mum. 'How could you let this happen?' I sobbed. 'How could you?' But as soon as I'd said it I was sorry. Mum was probably just as upset as we were.

We stayed with Mr and Mrs Bazley, who were very kind and looked after us as best they could.

Then one morning a lady in a brown hat and coat turned up. Mr Bazley brought her into the living room. 'Here they are. Linda...er, no, Lizzie and...er...' said Mr Bazley who had trouble remembering our names.

'I presume they've got their gas masks and cases and ration books, have they?' said the lady in brown.

Mr Bazley was easily confused. 'Oh, deary me. Cases? Ration books? Well, I don't know for sure. Florence will know, I...'

At that moment, Mrs Bazely walked into the living room; her eyes looked puffy as if she'd been crying. 'They've got no ration books,' she said. 'We've shared what we have and we've done what we can for the poor mites.'

'Quite so, Mrs Bazley,' the lady said, taking out a notebook. 'I shall have to organise some new ones.'

I thought I would be sick any minute. 'Where's she taking us?' I asked. 'Can't we stay here till Dad comes back?'

Mrs Bazley shook her head. 'Don't be upset, my lovely,' she said. 'They're going to find you a place where you'll be looked after properly.'

'But...'

She put her arm round my shoulders. 'I'm sure it won't be for long. They'll take care of you until your daddy comes back.'

'But you can take care of us, can't you?' I said.

Tears welled up in the old lady's eyes. 'I'm sorry, Lizzie,' she whispered, hugging me to her. 'You're fine children and your father would be very proud of you. I only wish...'

'The cases, Mrs Bazley,' said the lady in brown. 'We've a train to catch.'

Obediently, she scurried out of the room and returned with our case. 'They've just got the one. A few things that's all.'

The lady nodded and took two luggage labels from her handbag, hanging them around our necks. 'Just in case you get lost,' she said.

Tears were pouring down Mrs Bazely's wrinkled cheeks now.

'Come, Mrs Bazely,' said the lady in brown. 'Pull yourself together. You're much too old to look after these two, you know. Children of this age are quite a handful.'

'Yes, but...'

'It hasn't been easy to find them a billet, but we're hopeful that there are places available in South Wales.' Then she turned to us. 'Coats on now, children. Snap, snap.'

'You will be going with them, won't you?' asked Mrs Bazley, wiping her cheeks with a white handkerchief. 'They can't go all that way on their own.'

The lady in brown nodded. 'There'll be a teacher with other evacuees on that train. They're coming from Swindon, I think. I expect she'll look after them.'

Mrs Bazely would have come with us if she could. But the

lady wouldn't let her. 'You will write to us, won't you?' she said, trying to smile. 'We'll want to know you're all right.'

'We'll want to know you're all right,' Mr Bazely repeated, nodding his head. Then he pressed a silver sixpence into our hands while Mrs Bazley fetched a packet of sandwiches wrapped in brown paper and gave it to us.

'Come, come. No time to waste,' said the lady as she ushered us through the door and down the path to a small black car. As it moved off, we turned for one last look through the back window and waved to Mr and Mrs Bazely, who stood on the doorstep until we were out of sight.

'Don't be frightened, Freddie,' I whispered as I took hold of his hand. 'We're going to Wales. Dad wanted to go to Wales. Remember? He'll come for us soon. I know he will.' Freddie was shaking and, though I tried to sound brave for his sake, I was quaking, too, at the thought of us being on our own.

The lady in brown never spoke. I thought she might be sad. She had a solemn face and her mouth was set in a firm straight line. Perhaps her mum had been killed by a bomb too. You never know.

When she finally stopped the car, she said, 'Out you get. This is Gloucester station.' And she marched us to the ticket office then onto the platform. It was noisy and crowded with people, who were mostly dressed in uniform – some brown and some blue. One or two men had their wives and girl-friends with them, waiting to see them off. Some of them were kissing, which was very embarrassing so I looked away.

Normally, Freddie would have enjoyed being at a railway station. He loved trains and the noise and the excitement of it all. But not today. He stood, clinging onto my hand, his face pale and anxious. Poor Freddie.

'Don't worry,' I said. 'We'll find a nice place to stay and then we'll write Dad a letter. You'd like that, wouldn't you?'

He looked up at me. 'Where is Dad? Where did they take him?'

Before I could say that I didn't know, an announcement came over the Tannoy, booming round the station. '*The train now approaching platform two is the train for Fishguard, calling at...*'

There was a long list of place names I'd never heard of. Some of them were very strange as if they were in a foreign language. Nothing like Rochdale or Manchester or Oldham.

'Pick up your gas masks,' said the lady in brown. 'And your case. Quickly now.'

As we waited, the train pulled up with the grinding of wheels, the screeching of brakes and the long, loud hissing of steam. Those inside pulled down the windows and leaned out to see what was going on. Doors banged open, and people on the platform rushed towards the train in a great stampede.

We watched as they jostled to climb on board, while the lady in brown looked up and down the platform. Towards the back of the train, another woman was leaning out of the window, waving at us. 'Over here!' she called, and we were dragged along the platform towards her carriage.

'Are you with the school party from Swindon?' asked our lady in brown.

143

The lady on the train nodded.

'I've got two evacuees here to go to South Wales.' And she pushed us forward.

I never thought we were evacuees. What with the label and everything, I felt more like a piece of luggage.

The lady in the train smiled and held out her hand. 'Come on, you two,' she said, helping us up the steps. 'Don't worry. I'll see that you get there safely.'

By the time we were on board, the woman in the brown coat had already gone.

After that, I never did like brown coats – they always reminded me of that miserable, miserable day.

Twenty-Five

The train was crammed full of people. Even the corridor was packed with men in uniform, some sitting on kit bags.

'This is our carriage,' said the lady as she pulled aside the sliding door. 'We're a bit squashed, I'm afraid. But come in.' She tilted her head to read the labels round our necks. 'I'm Miss Trevor and I see that you are Lizzie and Freddie.'

We nodded.

'Freddie, you can sit on my knee, if you like,' she said. He didn't say anything, but when she picked him up, he didn't complain. 'Will you sit on your case for a while, Lizzie? Can you manage that?'

'I don't mind standing,' I said.

A boy near the door said, 'You can have my seat.'

I shook my head. I was too miserable to take any favours that day.

Miss Trevor tried to be nice to us. 'We're going to Llanelli in South Wales. It's very beautiful there and you'll be by the sea. I expect you'll enjoy that, won't you?'

But I shrugged and turned away because I didn't feel like chatting. I pressed my forehead against the door so my glasses dug into the bridge of my nose and hurt. That was nothing. The hurt inside was much, much worse.

I stared through the glass into the corridor. Soldiers were

leaning out of the window smoking Woodbines and laughing and talking. I wondered why they looked so happy when they were going to war. I didn't understand.

Some time later, Miss Trevor tapped me on the shoulder. 'I'm going to stretch my legs,' she said. 'Have my seat, Lizzie. I'm sure there's enough room for you and Freddie.'

She slid open the door into the corridor and stepped out. The men in uniform immediately turned to look at her and made silly whoops and cries.

'Hi, beautiful!' 'How ya doin'?' 'What a doll!'

The twang of American accents took me by surprise. 'Are they Yankies?' I asked a boy in a Fair Isle jumper.

'Course they are,' he said. 'Haven't you ever been to the pictures?' He folded his arms in a superior kind of way. 'A lot of 'em are film stars.'

'Oh!' I said.

The boy leaned forward. 'Some of them are really famous. Guess who I saw down the other end of the train this morning?'

'Who?'

'Only Johnny Weissmuller!'

'Who's he?'

'Don't you know nothink? He's Tarzan. He's been in hundreds of films. I nearly asked for his autograph but I decided not to.'

Some of the kids jeered at him. 'You're a right fibber, Colin Patterson,' said a girl with plaits and a pretty blue dress. 'You're always making up stories.'

When Miss Trevor came back, she stood outside in the

corridor talking to the Yankies. There was a lot of laughing going on, until I saw her look at her watch and she slid open the carriage door and stepped inside. 'Time to get out your packed lunches, children.'

I pulled Mrs Bazley's little parcel out of my pocket and peeled back the brown paper. I nudged Freddie who had fallen asleep. 'Wake up,' I said. 'Look, I've got our sandwiches.'

He opened his eyes. 'Not hungry.' He pushed me away, and then he started crying again. 'Don't want sandwiches. I want Dad.'

'Where is your dad?' asked the girl with the plaits. 'Is he in the army?'

I shook my head. 'No. He's a conscientious objector.'

'I've heard of them,' she said as she bit into her own sandwich. 'My mum told me.'

Miss Trevor tried to comfort Freddie. 'Never mind, little man,' she said, and she slipped off her coat and wrapped it round him like a blanket. 'You snuggle down next to Lizzie and have a nice sleep. We'll soon be there.'

After we'd finished our sandwiches, some of the kids fell asleep. Miss Trevor sat with a small girl on her lap and she nodded off too.

Except for me, only Colin Paterson and the girl with the plaits – who was called Shirley – were still awake and talking.

'My daddy built an Anderson shelter in the garden. It was the best one in our street. It had three beds in it and even an electric light!'

'That's nothing,' said Colin Patterson. 'In Islington, we took our bedding down the underground every night after school. We could hear the Jerry bombs boom...boom... boom...all night, but they couldn't get us down there, see. It was brilliant. We all sang songs and that.'

'If it was so great,' said Shirley, 'why did you get evacuated then?'

Colin shifted in his seat. 'I wanted to stay but Dad said it was too dangerous. He should know – he's a fire watcher. He's fantastic! He has to stand on the roof of Saint Paul's watching for incendiary bombs and—'

'So what?' Shirley interrupted. 'We had a bombing raid on Swindon and the corner shop where we bought our sweets got hit and Mrs West was buried in all the rubble.'

I wanted to put my fingers in my ears. It reminded me too much of Mum. I didn't want to listen.

'What about all the sweets?' asked Colin.

'They were buried, I think.'

'Didn't you look for 'em? There must have been loads.'

'No. They wouldn't let us.'

They were quiet for a while – even Colin. So I asked Shirley, who was sitting next to me, if she knew what would happen to us when we got off the train.

'Yes, I do, as a matter of fact,' she said. 'My mummy told me that there would be people waiting to take us to their homes. She said I was sure to get picked by somebody nice and probably rich because I'm pretty and I'm wearing my best blue dress and cardigan.'

148

'Picked?' I said. 'You mean they pick us like vegetables at the greengrocers.'

'Yes, and I'll tell you this for nothing' – she lowered her voice and nodded at a boy sitting near to the door – 'he won't get picked.'

'Why not?'

'Cos he's had his head shaved, hasn't he?'

'What's that got to do with it?'

'That means he had lice. Nobody wants a boy with lice.' Shirley smoothed her frock over her knees, making sure there were no creases and then she clasped her hands neatly in her lap and smiled a self-satisfied smile.

If that was true, who would want Freddie and me? I thought as the train chugged on. *What chance had we? Our clothes were in a real state and I had never been very pretty.* I pushed my glasses up my nose, leaned my head back and tried not to think about it. Instead, I listened to the clickety-clack of the wheels and my lids soon grew heavy and closed. When I opened them again, we were pulling into Llanelli station. I sat up and looked out of the window as the train came to a grinding stop.

Twenty-Six

Miss Trevor ushered us off the train, bleary-eyed and yawning, onto the platform. 'We have to go into the town,' she told us as we followed her out of the station to where the green trolleybus was waiting. None of us had ever seen one before, and we pushed and jostled to climb on board.

'Can we go upstairs, miss?' called Colin Patterson, who didn't wait for a reply but clattered up the metal steps.

When Miss Trevor said yes, we all followed Colin. I sat with Freddie looking down at the buildings as the trolleybus took us into the town centre. After a while, it pulled up near to a big building which was the town hall.

'Careful, children,' said Miss Trevor as we stampeded down the stairs. 'Make a nice line, please, and follow me.'

Once we were on the pavement, we walked behind her, our chins up, swinging our arms as smart as any soldier.

A man in a black suit was waiting for us in the doorway of the town hall. Miss Trevor held out her hand. 'Nice to meet you, Mr Jenkins,' she said. 'I hope we're not late.'

'No, no. Not at all,' he answered, shaking her hand so vigorously that I thought it would drop off. 'You're very welcome to Llanelli.' His voice was so loud that we could hear every word – even at the back of the queue. 'We've done what we can to find homes for the children but we already have

150

evacuees here, as I said to the billeting officer. Nobody's got any room, see. But come this way.'

He led us into a huge hall with wooden panels round the walls and a ceiling so high I could hardly see the top.

'Look,' said Freddie, pointing to a long table. 'There's lemonade, Lizzie. Is it for us? Is it?'

Miss Trevor overheard and told us it was, then took us over to the table. This was brilliant because we were all very thirsty after the train ride.

Shirley was first to drain her glass. 'I was right,' she said, wiping her mouth with the back of her hand. 'They're waiting for us. Look!' She pointed to the far end of the hall, where a group of people was standing watching us and chatting like farmers at a market.

Mr Jenkins came over and stood in front of us. 'Right now, children,' he said. 'I want you to line up against the wall over there so that these people can take a good look at you.'

I hated the idea. I was scared. But what could I do? I held Freddie's hand and shuffled across the hall with the other kids, walking in a line like a flock of sheep.

It happened just like Shirley said. People came and stared at us. Some of them smiled, some of them nodded and sniffed and prodded and asked how old we were, before they moved on to the next one.

It was no surprise who was picked first. Shirley stood there smiling like an angel and a lady in a coat with a fur collar and red lipstick came right up to her. 'You will do nicely,' she said.

'Come along, dear.' And they went off together, Shirley looking very pleased with herself.

The next to go were the two oldest and biggest boys. They were taken by a man with a weather-beaten face. 'Bet he's a farmer,' said Colin Patterson who was standing next to me. 'He'll have 'em workin' all day and all night. You see if I ain't right. Glad he didn't pick me.'

One by one, the others were chosen until there was only Freddie and me and the boy with the shaved head. Even he went. He was chosen by a bald man who obviously didn't care about him having no hair – so that left just the two of us.

I was beginning to think that nobody wanted Freddie and me, when a fat lady with a red hat and bright pink cheeks walked over to Freddie.

'I'll take the little boy,' she called to Mr Jenkins. 'I've just got a small room. He'll have to make do.'

She took hold of his hand, but Freddie yelled, 'No! I'm not going without Lizzie.'

The lady looked down at him and frowned. And when I grabbed Freddie's arm and pulled him away from her, she looked even more put out.

'He's not going by himself. He's with me. He's my brother.'

'Is he indeed?' she said. 'Well, I've no room for you, my girl. You'll just have to visit when you can. There's a war on, you know.'

She snatched Freddie out of my grip.

'You're not having him!' I yelled, and I lunged at her, clinging onto her sleeve and kicking out at her ankle.

'Stop it, Lizzie!' Miss Trevor called as she and Mr Jenkins came rushing towards us. 'Lizzie!' she shouted again as she pulled me away.

'I'm sorry,' said Mr Jenkins to the lady in the red hat. 'The children are tired, I'm afraid.'

She grunted and brushed her coat down with one hand but still held onto Freddie with the other. Then without a word, he bent over and sank his teeth into her hand. 'Aaggghhhh!' She screamed so loud that everyone turned to look. '*Aaggghhh!*' she screamed again, pulling her injured hand away. 'You vicious little animal!'

Before Mr Jenkins could make more apologies, she marched out of the hall flushed with embarrassment, her face having turned the same colour as her hat.

I hugged Freddie, and we clung together, shaking and sobbing until a small lady with brown hair and a black wool coat came over to us.

'Now then,' she said in a soft Welsh voice. 'Things might not be so bad. Let's see if you can dry those tears, shall we?'

I took off my glasses and rubbed them dry with the edge of my skirt. Freddie stopped crying, too, and looked up at her.

'Well, you're a fine pair, aren't you?' she said, putting her hands gently on our shoulders. 'You certainly know how to stick together. I like that.'

I must have looked surprised because she suddenly smiled at me. A beautiful smile it was. Warm and kind.

'I think I could manage the two of you,' she said. 'Would you like to come home with me?'

And that was the start of our stay in a village called Pwll with a family called Roberts.

Twenty-Seven

The pavements outside the town hall were covered in a layer of melting snow.

'The bus is over there, look,' Mrs Roberts said, pointing down the road. 'If we hurry we'll just catch it.'

We all ran and climbed on board. I sat next to Freddie, holding his hand and feeling scared because we were going to a place with a strange name with someone we didn't know. Dad was gone and we didn't know where he was. That was the worst thing. Not knowing.

As miserable as we were though, we liked Mrs Roberts straight away.

'Call me Auntie Katie,' she said, smiling her wide, warm smile. 'We'll be home in twenty minutes and there's a nice tea waiting for you. I expect you're starving. Long journey, was it?'

We didn't say much on the bus but Auntie Katie didn't seem to mind. She just kept chatting to us, pointing to the ships coming into the harbour and then to the railway that ran between the road and the sea.

'We get a lot of trains,' she said as one streaked past carrying coal and billowing smoke. 'You'll like watching them, I expect. All the children do it round here. The drivers wave to you, see. I did it myself when I was a girl.'

Her house was at the end of a long row of identical houses overlooking the sea. It was nothing like Rochdale. There were no factories that I could see. No tall chimneys. No smoke.

As we reached the house, a girl came running out from next door.

'Mammy! You're back,' she called. 'Auntie Alice saw you coming down the road.' Then she looked at us and stopped in her tracks. 'But you've got two, Mammy! I thought we were only having one.'

Auntie Katie smiled. 'Lizzie and Freddie come as a pair,' she said. 'Don't you worry – we'll manage.' And then she turned to us and said, 'This is my daughter, Joy, and she had her twelfth birthday only last week. She's a real chatterbox, if ever there was one. You might need some cotton wool in your ears if she gets too much for you.'

Joy grinned. 'Come on. I'll show you your room.' She led us down the hall and up the stairs. 'You've got a wardrobe and everything, see.' She opened a door on the landing. 'And Daddy's painted the walls too. It's ever so nice.'

Our bedroom was at the back of the house.

'It's dark now,' said Joy, closing the curtains. 'But tomorrow you'll be able to see out to the hills. Lovely, they are. I go up there walking with Daddy.'

The room was bigger than the one we'd built at Arthur's house and it was painted yellow, with a picture of a vase of roses hanging over the bed.

'You can put your things in the chest of drawers, see,' said Joy, before running to the top of the stairs and shouting,

'Mammy! Mammy! Have you forgotten there's only one bed?'

Auntie Katie called back. 'Auntie Marged's got a camp bed,' she said. 'I'll ask your father to go and pick it up when he gets home. Now hurry down and have some tea. Lizzie and Freddie are hungry.'

We followed Joy down the stairs and along the hall.

'Who's that?' I whispered as we passed a silver-framed photo of a man in uniform.

'It's my big brother, Gwilym,' she said. 'He's fighting the Germans in France. Mammy worries about him but I tell her he'll be all right because he's very clever.'

The kitchen was warm. There was a coal fire glowing in an iron grate and the smell of baking coming from the oven at the side. My mouth watered at the thought of food – especially when I saw the table, which was covered with plates of ham and tongue and pickles and cheese and Welsh cakes.

'A special treat,' said Auntie Katie, and I wondered if there was rationing in Wales. I hadn't seen so much food on one table – ever!

We were just sitting down to eat when we heard a rattle at the back door.

'That'll be your Uncle Ossie,' Auntie Katie told us.

Joy leaped up and ran to her father as he walked in. He had thick dark hair streaked with white and, although he wasn't tall, he looked strong, with square shoulders and a barrel chest.

'Well, well, well,' he said, smiling. 'Who have we here, Joy?'

'This is Lizzie and Freddie and they're evacuees and they've come to stay, and do you know we need another bed in the spare room and—'

'Whoa, my girl! Not so fast. Let me get my boots off and have a cup of tea, then I'll sort it all out.' He sat on the armchair in the corner of the kitchen and untied his laces. 'That's better,' he said, dropping his boots on the hearth before standing to reach a tobacco pouch off the mantelpiece.

'So,' he said, turning with his back to the fire and lighting his pipe, 'where do you fine children come from? London, is it?'

I shook my head. 'No. Rochdale.'

'Near Manchester?'

'Yes.'

'Well, I'm surprised they sent you all the way down here. Couldn't they find somewhere nearer to home?'

I looked down at my hands. 'No,' I said, barely above a whisper.

He pulled up a chair and sat at the table with us. 'That's a shame,' he said. 'Most young-uns like their parents to visit once in a while. Rochdale will be too far for them to come, see.'

Freddie, who had been sitting quietly, looked more miserable than ever. His bottom lip began trembling and his eyes filled. I gripped his hand under the table but that didn't stop the tears rolling down his cheeks and dripping off the end of his chin.

Auntie Katie hurried over and put her arms around him. 'There, there. Everything will be all right, you'll see. I expect you're missing your mammy and daddy, aren't you? It's only natural.'

At the words, 'mammy and daddy' Freddie broke into heart-wrenching sobs, and I felt my own tears well up, too.

Auntie Katie rocked him backwards and forward. 'Just think,' she said. 'They sent you here because they wanted you to be safe. You'll see them soon, you mark my words.'

Which made things even worse. Freddie howled like a cat with a trapped tail.

I swallowed back my tears and forced myself to explain. 'Our mum was killed when they dropped a bomb on her shop.'

Auntie Katie looked at me, open-mouthed. 'Oh, you poor things,' she cried. 'And I suppose your daddy's in the army.'

I shook my head slowly. 'No. The police took him away because he wouldn't fight in the war. We don't know where he is.'

Auntie Katie looked as if the breath had been knocked out of her. 'This gets worse,' she exclaimed. 'You mean they didn't tell you where they were taking him?'

I shook my head.

She looked across at her husband. 'Ossie, this is shameful. These children need to know where their daddy is, and he needs to know where *they* are.' Then she stood up and took her coat off the hook. 'I'm going back to Llanelli. I'll make sure that billeting officer does something about this, or my name's not Katie Roberts.'

'You're too late, Katie,' said Uncle Ossie. 'He'll have gone home for his tea.'

But she was already buttoning her coat. 'Then I'll go to his house. I've known Ivor Jenkins since we were at school,' she said as she put on her hat. 'I won't let him rest until he's done something about this, see if I don't.'

She walked out, slamming the front door and leaving the house silent until Uncle Ossie stood up. 'Well, that's that, then. Poor Ivor Jenkins will have a terrible time unless he does what Katie says – you mark my words.'

Freddie stopped crying and wiped away his tears.

'We'd better make ourselves busy while she's away,' said Uncle Ossie, and he tapped his pipe on the grate and put it back on the mantelpiece. 'Finish your teas and then let's go up to Auntie Marged's to get that bed.' He looked at Freddie and smiled. 'By the time we've done that, I expect Auntie Katie will be home with some news of your daddy.' Then he picked my brother up and held him high above his head. 'Touch the ceiling for luck, Freddie,' he said, and as Freddie reached up, he smiled for the first time that day.

Twenty-Eight

Before we went to bed, Auntie Katie came back.

'What did Mr Jenkins say?' I asked. 'You did see him, didn't you?'

'Well,' said Auntie Katie, sitting in the armchair by the fire. 'He was having his tea but I told him, "Look here, Ivor Jenkins, I've got two children who are very upset and need to know where their daddy is. What are you going to do about it?" Well, he didn't like having his meal interrupted and he said he would go back to the town hall when he'd finished. But I stood over him and watched every last mouthful and then I went with him while he rang some people in Stroud.'

'So what did they say? Where have they taken Dad?'

Auntie Katie pulled Freddie onto her lap. 'They said they'd have some news tomorrow. So you don't have to worry, see. I'll go back to Ivor Jenkins first thing in the morning.'

Freddie screwed up his face. 'I want my dad now,' he cried and, in spite of more hugs from Auntie Katie, he was really unhappy that night.

We lay cuddled up together even though we had fetched the second bed from Auntie Marged's house. We lay there thinking about Dad in a horrible cell and wondering when we would see him again.

Once Freddie was asleep, I slipped out of bed and went across to the window. But the sky was covered in cloud that night so there were no stars and it seemed that I had lost Mum too. Was it any wonder that I felt more miserable than ever?

The next morning, Joy burst into our bedroom. 'Come on, you two,' she said. 'We're going out with Daddy this morning. We're going up to the woods.'

'Haven't you got to go to school?'

'No, silly. It's the Christmas holidays, isn't it? We're going to get the tree and then we'll put it in the parlour and hang the decorations on it. It'll be fun. Come on.'

That first morning, we got dressed and went downstairs where Uncle Ossie was finishing his breakfast.

Freddie sat at the table and peered into his face. 'You aren't a soldier, are you?' he asked.

Uncle Ossie finished scraping his bowl and smiled. 'No. I'm not a soldier.'

'Daddy's a pilot,' Joy said as she sat next to him.

I stared. A pilot? I couldn't believe it. Uncle Ossie didn't look like one. He was too old for one thing and he didn't have a uniform.

'What kind of planes do you fly?' I asked.

Joy burst out laughing. 'No. He's not that kind of pilot.'

'Let me explain,' he said. 'I go out to big ships in the bay, see. Then I climb out of the pilot boat onto the ship and bring it down the estuary and into the docks at Llanelli. It can be tricky if you don't know these parts, what with the sand banks and the currents. You can soon be in trouble. The pilot has to show 'em the way.'

'You must be very important,' said Freddie.

'Oh yes. I look after the ships carrying steel and coal, and the government would rather I did that than join the army.'

'And you won't have to fight?'

'No, I won't. So don't you worry, son,' he said, standing up. 'Now let's get the porridge and you can have your breakfast.' He reached for three bowls off a shelf then went over to the stove. 'Auntie Katie's gone off to Llanelli to pester Ivor Jenkins again.'

'Will she find out about Dad?'

'She'll follow Ivor Jenkins like a shadow,' Uncle Ossie said as he ladled porridge out of the pan. 'I'm telling you, boy, she won't give up till he gives her some answers. Poor man. I feel sorry for him. Really I do.'

He put the bowls in front of us on the table.

'Mammy's porridge is the best,' said Joy as we started to eat. 'She's a brilliant cook, isn't that right, Daddy?'

What I remember most about Auntie Katie's house was the kitchen. We spent most of our time there, and there was always a fire in the grate and the smell of something tasty in the oven.

'You ready for a trip out this morning?' Uncle Ossie asked, ruffling Freddie's hair. 'When you've finished your porridge, we'll go up to the wood and find that Christmas tree. I've no work today so that's all right. Coats on, mind. It's nippy out there this morning.'

The wind blowing off the sea was bitterly cold and brought rain that washed away the remains of the snow. We put on our coats and scarves, and Joy wore a shiny red raincoat with a matching sou'wester, and Uncle Ossie carried a saw.

Every Christmas in Rochdale, we took our little artificial tree off the top of the wardrobe. It had been there all year ever since the January before. Even though it had been wrapped in newspaper and was covered in a layer of dust, we loved it. But fetching a *real* tree was something new to us.

The four of us climbed up the hill with the wind and rain striking our faces, but once we were in the wood it wasn't so bad. Uncle Ossie walked in front of us with the saw in his hand, searching for the right kind of tree. I looked everywhere, this way and that, but I couldn't see one. Most of them were bare except for the fir trees, which were as tall as houses and much too big for us.

Suddenly, he stopped. 'Here, look you. This is a fine old tree. It will do us very nicely, eh, Joy? Which bit do you think?'

Uncle Ossie was standing in front of a holly tree and we watched, puzzled, as Joy pointed to a branch. Then he sawed it off, slung it over his shoulder and we all headed back down the hill.

'I thought we were getting a tree,' I said to Joy. 'Why did you cut the holly?'

She raised her eyebrows and giggled. 'That's our Christmas tree, silly. It'll look ever so pretty when we've put the decorations on it. Just you see.'

Back at the house, the holly branch was put in a pot full of soil and carried into the parlour. Uncle Ossie fetched a box of decorations from the loft and we took them out one by one and hung them on the branches. We got scratched more than once – but it didn't matter.

'This is my most favourite one,' said Joy, holding up a lighthouse made of cardboard. 'Just watch.' She took the wire hanging from it and pushed a plug into a socket on the wall.

Freddie squealed. 'It lights up!' he said, holding out his hand to touch it. 'How did it do that?'

'It's electric, see,' said Joy. 'We got electricity last year. Only downstairs, mind. But Auntie Marged's got it upstairs as well *and* she's got a bathroom. She lets me have a bath on Fridays. You can share mine, if you like, Lizzie.'

By the time we'd decorated the tree, Auntie Katie had come back from seeing Ivor Jenkins. She had hardly taken her coat off when I ran into the kitchen to ask about Dad. 'Is there any news, Auntie Katie?'

'Well,' she said, opening her handbag and taking out a piece of paper. 'I have your father's address for you, and I've also made sure that Ivor Jenkins has sent our address to your father.'

She handed me the paper. Freddie stood by me, quivering with excitement while I unfolded it. At the top was Dad's name followed by some numbers. Underneath were the words:

Wormwood Scrubs Prison
Du Cane Road
London

Twenty-Nine

Dear Dad,

We have just got your address. Hurray! I hope this arrives before Christmas Day because we want to wish you HAPPY CHRISTMAS.

We miss you a lot and hope you won't be in that horrible place for long. Freddie has drawn you a picture of us just so you don't forget us! Can't write more or I'll miss the post but I'll write a really long letter next time.

Lots and lots of love and hugs from,

Lizzie and Freddie

XXXXXXXXXXXXXXXXXXXXXXXXXXXXX

ps. We are with a very nice family and have good things to eat.

DEAR DAD,
PLEASE COME AND GET US SOON.
PLEASE PLEASE PLEASE PLEASE.

LOVE FROM FREDDIE

We put our address on the envelope so Dad would know it was from us even before he opened it. Auntie Katie gave us a stamp and we raced down to the pillar box just in time for the next collection.

'Well now,' said Auntie Katie, when we got back, 'I expect there'll be a letter for you after Christmas.'

'How long will that be?' asked Freddie.

'A few days,' said Auntie Katie. 'But we've got a lot of things to do before then. We've got the mince pies to make and the stuffing, and the vegetables to dig out of the garden.'

Freddie wasn't interested in the cooking. He went and fetched a paper and pencil off the sideboard and said, 'I'm going to write to Father Christmas.'

Auntie Katie smiled and winked at him. 'I've been thinking about that, Freddie,' she said. 'You should write him a note telling him where you are. We don't want him driving round on his sleigh looking for you, do we?'

While he was writing, Auntie Marged walked in carrying a large bundle. She was Auntie Katie's sister and they looked so alike that they could have been twins – except that Auntie Marged's hair was silver white and Auntie Katie's was brown. 'I've been sorting out some clothes,' she said, dumping her bundle on the armchair. 'Our Enid and Hugh have outgrown these. So you can have them if you like, Lizzie and Freddie. They might suit.'

They did suit. It was wonderful to have a dress that covered my knees and a coat with sleeves that went all the way down to my wrists.

For the next few days we were busy getting ready for Christmas. I helped Joy make the longest paper chain in the world and we laughed as we hung it round the parlour. Even though I missed Dad like mad, Joy made me feel almost happy. She was like the sister I had always wanted and we had a good time together.

While we were doing the decorations, Freddie was sitting at the kitchen table, a pencil in his hand and his tongue gripped between his teeth as he wrote more letters to Father Christmas.

'Come and help us, Freddie,' I'd say, but he would shake his head and write yet another letter to throw up the chimney.

On Christmas Eve, Joy had her hair all done up in rags.

'Would you like me to do yours, Lizzie?' Auntie Katie asked.

'No thanks,' I said. I didn't want my hair curled, even though it was a special Christmas dinner the next day and I'd be wearing the new dress. I wasn't keen on curls.

When we were ready to go to bed, Auntie Katie went to the cupboard in the corner and pulled out three large grey socks. 'You'll be needing these to hang up,' she said, giving us one each. 'Take them upstairs and see what Father Christmas brings, eh?'

But Freddie's eyes suddenly misted over and his bottom lip quivered. 'Dad won't have a stocking in prison. I know he won't.'

Uncle Ossie took him on his knee. 'Then just supposing we give you an extra one,' he said. 'And you can keep the presents safe and give them to your daddy when he comes to see you. How's that?'

Auntie Katie fetched another sock, and Freddie smiled and took it upstairs. We hung our stockings over the little fireplace in our bedroom – one for Freddie, one for me and one for Dad. Joy went into her bedroom and did the same.

We didn't go to sleep straight away. Joy came and perched on the edge of my bed.

'What do you think we'll get in our stockings?' she said. 'I'm hoping I'll get a picture of Shirley Temple.'

'Why would you want a picture of Shirley Temple?'

'To hang on my wall,' she said. 'I want to be like her. All pretty and in the films, and singing and that.' She sighed. 'But then I wouldn't mind a book.'

Freddie, who had been sitting cross-legged in his bed, suddenly said, 'How does Father Christmas know what to give Dad?'

Joy looked at him. 'Father Christmas has a present for everybody and I'm sure he'll know exactly what's right for your daddy.' And she winked across at me.

'But *how* will he?' asked Freddie.

She shrugged her shoulders. 'In my experience, Father Christmas knows everything and he always waits until I've gone to sleep before he comes down the chimney.'

But Freddie's cheeks flushed with anger. 'If Father Christmas is so clever, why didn't he get Dad out of prison? I wrote to ask him a hundred times but he didn't, did he?'

He flung himself face down onto his bed.

'Freddie,' I said. 'Dad will be OK, I promise. Now go to sleep, and when you wake up, there'll be presents for all of us.'

I knew he didn't care about presents. Neither did I. We both wanted the same thing for Christmas. Our dad.

Thirty

I was woken in the middle of the night with the feeling that someone was moving about. I heard the curtains being pulled back, and when I opened my eyes, the room was flooded with a strange pink light.

I turned my head and saw Freddie standing by the window, looking out.

'What are you doing?' I said, putting on my glasses.

He spun round, his eyes wild with excitement. 'Lizzie, it's Father Christmas!'

'No, Freddie. Father Christmas won't come if you're awake. Remember what Joy told us?'

He shook his head and frowned. 'Well, Joy was wrong because he *has* come.' Then he pointed out of the window. 'Come and see.'

When I went to look, I saw that beyond the trees, on the far side of the hill, the sky was filled with a red glow.

'He's there,' Freddie insisted. 'You can see the lights on his sleigh.'

I pressed my nose against the glass, trying to make out what it was. When I turned round to speak, Freddie was getting dressed.

'What are you doing?' I asked. 'It's the middle of the night.'

'I'm going to see Father Christmas,' my brother said,

pulling on his trousers. 'If I can talk to him and tell him about Dad, he'll do something. I know he will. Perhaps he didn't get my letters.'

Before I could stop him, Freddie had bolted out of the door and down the stairs. All I could do was fling on my own clothes and go after him.

By the time I reached the back door he was well ahead. 'Wait for me, Freddie,' I called as I pulled on my coat. I could see him racing up the path towards the red glow, but he was in such a tizzy that he hadn't put his coat on. So I grabbed it off the hook and took it with me.

His legs couldn't keep going for ever and I caught up with him halfway up the hill and made him put his coat on. We went on together to the top and it was then that we saw what was making the bright light. Sparks were flying high into the night and we both gawped in amazement. We hadn't expected to see trees on fire, or a wreckage in the woods, or blazing mangled metal.

'It's a plane,' said Freddie. 'It's crashed.'

I pushed my glasses up my nose, staring and trying to see beyond the flames and the smoke. 'Look over there on the ground,' I said, pointing to something a little way from the aircraft. 'I think it's the pilot. He must be injured.'

'Let's go and help him. Come on!' Freddie shouted, and he ran towards the body, his legs slipping and sliding while I followed behind.

I didn't like what I saw. The man had been thrown clear of the plane. He was lying on the ground, with blood trickling down the side of his face and his uniform torn and burned in parts. I grabbed hold of Freddie to slow him down and we moved forward together until we were closer to the injured man. I thought he might be dead and I leaned over to see if he was still breathing.

Then it happened so suddenly that we leaped back in surprise. The man's eyes shot open and he stared at us. We froze on the spot as he raised his hand and wiped the blood from his face. Then he groaned and tried to move but he couldn't. '*Pomóż mi,*' he moaned. '*Pomóż mi.*'

I gasped when I heard him. 'That's not English,' I said. 'He's a Jerry. Freddie! Oh heavens! We've caught a German. He crashed his plane and now he's in Wales. There might be more of them. We've got to get help. Quick.'

'*Jestem ranny,*' the man said, holding out his hand towards us.

I pushed Freddie away. 'Go back to the house. Run as fast as you can and tell Uncle Ossie. Now, Freddie. Go now!'

But Freddie stood and stared. 'Is he the German that dropped that bomb on Mum? Is it him, Lizzie? Is it?'

'No, I don't expect he's the same one,' I said. 'But don't just stand there, Freddie. Go and tell Uncle Ossie to get the police!' And as he started to run I shouted, 'Tell him to call the army too!'

While Freddie raced back, I kept my eyes fixed on the German. His head was cut open and his hand was injured but he was moving a little bit. *What if he had a gun? Or what if he suddenly got up and ran off and brought more Jerries?* My knees began to knock at the thought of it. He was the enemy. Whatever happened, I mustn't let him get away.

I looked for inspiration but found none until I noticed the scarf around his neck. Then I had an idea. With my heart hammering against my ribs, I took a step forward and leaned over him. He looked up at me, staring with eyes so wide and wild that I thought he might have superhuman powers and grab hold of me. But, before he could do anything, I snatched the scarf and stepped back out of reach. Then I crouched down by his feet and wrapped it tight around his ankles, tying it in a knot.

There was no way the German could undo that, I was sure. His hand was too badly injured. Now I would wait and watch him until Uncle Ossie arrived. I just hoped he wouldn't be long.

I stood straining to hear his footsteps coming up the hill, but there was nothing. Only the wind whistling through the dried bracken and the bare branches of the trees. The minutes dragged by. It seemed like hours, and my heart beat so fast that I thought it would burst. But then I heard a voice. 'Lizzie! I'm here. I'm coming.'

Uncle Ossie suddenly appeared at the top of the hill, running, gasping, panting. 'Uncle Ossie!' I cried, charging over to him. 'A German bomber crashed and there's a pilot and I've captured him.'

He stopped in front of me, bending forward, hands on knees, trying to get his breath back. 'Lead...me...to...him,' he gasped, and put his hand on my shoulder. 'You've done well, my girl. Your Auntie Katie has gone for help. They'll be here soon.'

As we went down the other side of the hill I pointed to the wreck of the plane.

'That's a mess and no mistake,' he said, rubbing his chin. 'But it isn't a German plane. It's a Spitfire.'

'What's that?'

'A British fighter plane.'

'But…but the pilot was talking in German.'

'Where is he?'

I led him to the man lying on the ground. 'This is him,' I said.

He kneeled on the ground by the side of the pilot. 'Now then, boy,' he said. 'What's happened here?' And he began to untie the scarf and release the pilot's legs.

'Pembrey,' the man said, slowly. 'Pembrey.'

Uncle Ossie nodded his head. 'You are from Pembrey?' He spoke every word slowly and clearly. 'With the RAF?'

The man stared at him, then smiled a little and said, '*Tak*'.

Uncle Ossie looked up at me. 'No need to be frightened, Lizzie. We've not been invaded by the Germans,' he said. 'This man's a Polish pilot. There's quite a few of 'em stationed down the road at Pembrey RAF base. He must have been flying back to the base when he crashed, poor chap.'

Uncle Ossie looked at the pilot again and patted his arm gently. 'No worries, boy. We'll have you up to the hospital in no time.'

Thirty-One

Uncle Ossie learned that the pilot was called Piotr Ostrowski and the next morning everyone in the street and the whole of Pwll had heard what had happened.

Some came round and made a terrible fuss. 'Oh, how brave!' they said. 'How clever you were to find him and save his life.'

No one except Uncle Ossie knew my guilty secret – that I'd thought the pilot was a Jerry and I'd tied him up.

'Well, this is a fine old Christmas Day, isn't it?' said Auntie Katie as she took the chicken out of the oven. 'We've got a pair of little heroes in our house, eh, Joy?'

I think Joy was upset that she hadn't come with us – but she smiled anyway. So that was all right.

We ate Christmas dinner in the dining room, with Auntie Katie's best white cloth spread on the table. It was grand. Chicken all crisp and brown. Carrots and sprouts straight from Uncle Ossie's vegetable garden. And thick brown gravy.

Freddie didn't eat much. He sat there, his chin on his chest, looking miserable.

'What is it, Freddie?' asked Auntie Katie. 'Father Christmas came, didn't he? I saw those stockings of yours – bulging they were.'

Freddie nodded.

'You had that snakes and ladders game,' said Joy. 'We'll play afterwards, if you like.'

Freddie shrugged and managed to look even more miserable.

'You didn't have much sleep last night, did you, my little man?' said Auntie Katie. 'You were very brave saving that pilot.'

Freddie looked up and stared at her. 'But he wasn't a German, was he?'

'No. He was Polish.'

'I *wanted* him to be German,' said Freddie.

We all looked at each other, puzzled.

'Why?' I asked.

'Cos if we'd captured a German, the king would be very pleased and he would let Dad out of prison. That's why. But he was just a Polish man, so now Dad will have to stay in that horrible place. I *HATE* THIS WAR.'

He shoved back his chair, pushed Auntie Katie away and raced up the stairs. Then he flung himself on the bed and cried until he fell asleep, and stayed that way for most of the day.

Then it was Boxing Day and we were all going up to Auntie Marged's for tea. Freddie didn't want to go but I said that Dad would be cross if he didn't.

'All the family will be there,' said Joy. 'They're dying to meet you both.'

By half past three we were dressed in our best and walking up the road. Auntie Marged's house was so full of people you could hardly breathe. Every uncle, aunt and cousin had come to eat her Christmas tea, which was spread out on the table with her best china. It was very noisy, I remember. When we arrived, everybody seemed to be talking at once in Welsh, and we didn't understand. But once Uncle Ossie had announced our arrival we were the centre of attention and they spoke English.

'So this is Lizzie and Freddie, is it?' said an old man, who we learned was Great Uncle Ismael. He had a white beard and a big belly and twinkling eyes. 'You must tell us how you found that pilot. Exciting I'm sure.'

When we were full to bursting with all the cakes and mince pies, we told them about Piotr Ostrowski. Freddie was still in a bit of a sulk, so it was up to me to tell the story. I like telling stories but I sometimes exaggerate a bit. After all, nobody likes a boring tale. Anyway, when I'd told them about the whole dangerous adventure, discovering the blazing plane, saving the dying pilot and one or two other things that I won't bother you with, they all clapped and said nice things.

That was when the siren sounded.

'Well,' said Aunt Marged. 'Would you believe it? On Boxing Day, indeed!'

'Is there an Anderson shelter?' I asked Joy.

'There's one behind The Collier's Arms but we don't use it. We all go down the tunnel. Come on. Follow Mammy.'

I held Freddie's hand as we all walked out of the house and crossed the road.

'Where are we going?' I asked.

'Here, see.' Joy pointed to an opening that ran back under

the road and into the hillside. 'It's an old tunnel that leads to the mine. Much better than a silly old Anderson shelter. We're safe as anything down here.'

Some people shone torches inside the tunnel and I saw trucks that ran on rails.

'Climb in,' said Joy. 'You'll like it.'

Everybody climbed inside the trucks – except for a few of the men who pushed them. I suppose at one time they were used for carrying coal, but now they carried us down the tunnel until we were well away from the entrance.

Freddie had cheered up no end and he stood at the front of our truck, gripping the edge and calling, 'Faster! Faster!'

When we stopped and climbed out, we found we were in a space carved out of the rock. That was amazing enough. But even better was the fact that the floor was covered with carpets and there were settees and chairs to sit on.

'Everybody brings their old furniture down here,' said Joy. 'It makes it seem more homely. That's what Mammy says.'

Freddie took some persuading to get out of the truck, but Great Uncle Ismael lit the oil lamps and soon the space was glowing with a warm light. Eventually, Freddie went to sit on a comfy armchair with Auntie Katie.

'We're not going to let those Germans spoil our party,' said Aunt Marged. 'We'll sing some carols.'

We started with 'Away in a Manger' at full blast – loudest of all was Great Uncle Ismael with a voice deeper than a coal mine. Our voices echoed round the rock walls and it sounded so wonderful that we might have been in a cathedral.

We were down there for three or four hours, waiting for the all clear to sound. We sang a lot and talked a lot and I got to tell more stories. One of them had everybody rocking with laughter. It was about a mean old farmer who got his hand caught in a rat-trap ...

Thirty-Two

The following day we were all playing dominoes after tea, when there was a knock at the door and Joy ran down the passage to answer it. 'Mammy! It's Thomas Morgan. He says he's got something for you.'

It sounded exciting, so I followed Auntie Katie to see what it was. A boy in navy uniform was standing on the doorstep with an envelope in his hand. When Auntie Katie saw him, she stopped in her tracks and clapped her hand over her mouth. 'No!' she said. 'Oh, no!' She put her hand on the wall to steady herself and I thought she was going to faint. But she straightened her shoulders and walked towards the door.

Thomas Morgan didn't speak to her. He just held out an envelope and I remember how Auntie Katie's hand shook as she took it. Her face turned deathly white and she turned and walked back to the kitchen, dropping the envelope on the table as if it was a red-hot coal.

When Uncle Ossie saw it he closed his eyes for a second. Then he swallowed and took a deep breath before he reached for it. Slowly, slowly he pulled out the slip of paper, unfolded it and stared.

'What is it, Daddy?' said Joy. 'What's wrong?'

Uncle Ossie coughed to clear his throat before he read the short typed message out loud: '*The war ministry regrets to inform*

181

you that your son, Gwilym Roberts, has been reported lost in action.'

The telegram fell to the table as he reached for Auntie Katie's hand, but she snatched it away and let out a howl like a wolf in the wilderness. I shall never forget it. It was a terrible noise, so full of pain. Then the screaming started and the sobbing, and although Uncle Ossie put his arms around her and held her tight, he couldn't stop her shaking.

'Go upstairs, children,' he said softly. 'Katie's not well.'

'Let me stay, Daddy,' whispered Joy. 'I want to stay with Mammy.'

Uncle Ossie looked at her with pleading eyes. 'Just give us ten minutes, love. That's all.'

Reluctantly, we climbed the stairs, hoping that Uncle Ossie could make Auntie Katie better.

Joy's eyes were already brimming with tears. 'That telegram's probably a load of lies,' she said as she sat on the edge of my bed. 'Our Gwilym's not dead, you know. They make mistakes all the time. He'll come home, I know he will.' But when she couldn't hold back her tears any longer, she buried her head in her hands and sobbed.

I hugged her and rocked her backwards and forward, just like Mum used to do, until her tears had dried.

'Shall we play snakes and ladders for a bit?' I suggested.

'Oh yes!' said Freddie. 'And I'm going to win!'

But Joy didn't want to. 'I think I'll go and read my book,' she said, and went into her own bedroom. I thought I heard her crying. I felt like crying myself. But Freddie didn't really understand what the telegram meant and I was glad.

'If we're not going to play snakes and ladders,' he said, 'can we write to Dad?'

'Good idea. We'll make it a cheerful sort of letter, shall we? Don't want to make Dad feel miserable, do we?'

So I wrote the jolliest note I could.

Dear Dad,

We hope you got our first letter.

We had a nice Christmas except for missing you lots. We went to a party and everybody gave us sixpence except for Great Uncle Ismael who is very fat.

He gave us a shilling. We are saving our money so that we can come to visit you at the prison.

Freddie has done a picture for you to put on your wall.

Please write to us soon if you can.

Lots of love,
Lizzie and Freddie

DEAR DAD, PLEASE GET OUT OF PRISON AS SOON AS YOU CAN BECAUSE I MISS YOU LOTS AND LOTS AND LOTS.

FROM FREDDIE

After that telegram, Auntie Katie could only think of Gwilym – where he was, and if he was ever coming home. Uncle Ossie tried his best to cheer her up and so did Joy, but they were feeling miserable, too. Joy didn't want to talk about it and kept herself in her own room and that made me feel sad and lonely. The house felt different – cold and empty, as if something had been lost and would never be the same again.

Freddie was confused. Every now and then he tried to hug Auntie Katie but she'd push him away and say, 'Not now, Freddie.' So he became withdrawn and hardly spoke to anyone. I could understand why. He felt he had lost Mum and Dad, and now he had lost the lovely, smiling Auntie Katie. He started clinging to me, thinking I might leave him as well.

Then one night, I suddenly thought that there might be a way to make our lives better.

'What do you think, Freddie?' I said. 'How would you like to go back to Whiteway?'

He looked up at me, his eyes wide with hope. 'You mean live in Arthur's house again? In our bedroom? And play with Jip? And see Basil and Lalia and Bernardo?'

I smiled. 'We were happy there, weren't we? Shall we write and ask Arthur if we can stay until Dad comes home?'

'Oh, yes, Lizzie. Please! Can we?' He rushed to fetch some paper out of the sideboard and we went up to our bedroom and wrote this:

Dear Arthur,

Dad is in a horrible prison called Wormwood Scrubs and we have been sent to South Wales.

We are evacuees and Freddie is upset all the time. Please could we come and live with you till Dad gets out of prison? We won't do anything bad, and we'll help you all we can. We miss you and Lalia and Bernardo and Basil and Jip.

Love from Lizzie

PLEASE CAN WE COME TO LIVE WITH YOU AND JIP? PLEASE PLEASE PLEASE. I WILL BE VERY VERY GOOD.

FROM FREDDIE XXXXX

Thirty-Three

Time dragged, and there was no word from either Dad or Arthur. The Christmas holidays were soon over and Freddie started at the little school in Pwll.

He hated it.

'They talk funny,' he said after the first day. 'I don't understand them. Why can't they talk properly?'

'It's Welsh, Freddie,' I explained. 'And they don't talk Welsh all the time, do they? I expect you'll get used to it.'

'Can't you come to my school? I don't like it on my own.'

'I've got to go with the big-uns to Llanelli,' I explained. 'They won't let me go with you. I'm too old.'

I didn't like my school any more than Freddie liked his. Joy was there, and Shirley, the girl from the train, was there too. But most of the girls spoke in Welsh to each other and I felt left out. It was as if they were talking about me behind my back.

But my real problem was a gang of four evacuees from London. Shirley must have told them that Dad was a conscientious objector so they made my life a misery.

'Don't play with her,' they said. 'Her dad's a coward. We don't mix with her sort.'

I tried to ignore their nasty remarks and their accidentally-on-purpose bumps in the playground but every day it got worse. I could hear Dad saying, 'Walk away, Lizzie,' but one day my temper got the better of me. I felt my cheeks burning and I turned to face them. That was when the fight started. Hair tugging. Thumping. Kicking. Scratching. I took on all four of them.

'Stop it at once!' shouted our teacher, Miss Jones, as she raced across the playground. She grabbed my arm and shook me like a rag doll.

'You're a troublemaker, that's what you are. Go to the head's room.' I marched away from them into the school. There was no point in explaining that I was standing up for my family. Mum would be proud of me. I knew that.

Not long after, a letter arrived. There was no doubt about it — it was Dad's writing on the envelope.

I ran upstairs, flung myself onto my bed and slit the envelope open. Inside was a single piece of white paper which I unfolded very slowly because I wanted to make the moment last for as long as possible. It was as if Dad was in the room, waiting to talk to us. And yet I shivered, scared to hear what he had to say.

Freddie had followed me into the bedroom. 'It's from Dad, isn't it?' he said. 'Read it out, Lizzie.'

So I held the paper in front of me and spoke the words Dad had written:

Dear Lizzie and Freddie,

You have no idea how glad I am to have your letters. I read them every day, over and over, and I keep them under my pillow. I have stuck the pictures on the walls and I look at them all the time and think about you both.

I will be out of here at the end of April. So that isn't such a long time, is it? I have made a calendar and I cross off each day just before I go to sleep.

There are no real criminals in this prison, as they've been sent away, but there are lots of people in here who feel that war is wrong like I do. They are called pacifists and we all get along just grand. One of them is called Michael Tippet. He writes music and is quite famous. Two of his friends called Benjamin Britten and a singer called Peter Pears came and gave us a concert. It cheered us all up.

Prison is not a very nice place but I think about you all the time and that makes me happy.

Be good for me. It won't be long before we're together again.

Love from your dad.

xxxxx

'Again, Lizzie. Read it again,' said Freddie.

And after I'd read it for the second time and then for the third time, he looked at me and frowned as if there was something he couldn't understand. '*When* is Dad coming?' he asked.

'April. That's about three and a half months.'

'Three and a half months?' he said, staring wide-eyed and horrified. 'No, Lizzie, no! It's too long.'

There was nothing I could do to make the days pass quickly, but every night I spoke to Mum and asked her to help us get back to Whiteway.

'Just till Dad gets out of prison. Please,' I said. And she always twinkled back at me – so I knew she was going to try her best.

Then a letter arrived.

Dear Lizzie and Freddie,

Arthur was so pleased to hear from you and sends you lots of love. I'm sorry to say he has been ill since Christmas. I've been taking care of him, but he is an old man and he is not strong. However, he says that he will be very pleased for you to come to stay as soon as he is better.

Bernardo hopes you are both well and I know he misses you – as I do. I will come and visit you as soon as I can.

Love from,
Lalia, Bernardo and Arthur XXXXX

Arthur was ill. That was not what we wanted to hear. But if Lalia came down to visit us she might take us back to Whiteway.

All we had to do was wait.

Thirty-Four

The next Saturday, Uncle Ossie suggested we went to visit
Piotr Ostrowski in the hospital. 'Let's see how he's getting on,
shall we?' he said. 'I'm sure he'll be feeling better by now.'

It was nearly three weeks since the plane crash. I
remembered him lying on the ground, unable to move with
blood running down his face. I wondered what he would
look like now. Maybe he'd lost an eye. Maybe there was a big
black hole where it used to be. And what about his legs?

I had never been inside a hospital and the first thing I
noticed was the smell of disinfectant. The corridors were very
long and straight and painted cream and green.

It was ages before we found the ward where Piotr was. As
we walked in, Uncle Ossie stopped a nurse. 'Can you tell me
where Piotr Ostrowski is?'

She pointed to the far end. 'He's in the last bed,' she said.
'See?'

We walked down the ward between two rows of beds
with men sitting up wearing striped pyjamas. When we
reached the one the nurse had pointed to, we saw PIOTR
OSTROWSKI printed on a card and clipped on the end of the
bed.

He was propped up, half lying, half sitting, and his face was
grey and gaunt. He looked no better than he had three weeks

ago – except they'd cleaned off the blood. His left eye was covered with a pad and, although I looked hard, I couldn't see what was under it. As for his legs, they were hidden by the blankets so I didn't know if he still had two. And I didn't like to ask.

'Piotr,' said Uncle Ossie, leaning over him. 'I've brought the two children who found you after the crash.'

He looked at us, puzzled, and didn't reply.

'Uncle Ossie,' I said, 'he doesn't speak any English. Remember?'

The man in the next bed reached out and tapped my arm. 'I can help,' he said. And he looked across at Piotr and said, '*Te dzieci znalały ciebje w lesie.*'

A smile spread slowly across Piotr's face and he leaned forward and grasped Uncle Ossie's hand and then ours, saying, '*Dziekuje*' over and over.

Freddie stared at the pilot. 'I think he must be Welsh. That's why he's talking funny.' He turned to the man in the next bed. 'Is he speaking Welsh?'

The man laughed. 'No. Not Welsh. He is a very important person from Poland. He speaks Polish like me.'

From then on, the man in the next bed did all the translating. We would ask a question and then he would say it in Polish to Piotr.

He told us that his friend's eye was going to be all right and he still had two legs – which was good news. We learned that Piotr had two children called Aurek and Alkaand; he pulled a photograph out of his pyjama pocket and showed us. He looked very sad because he had not seen them or their mother for two years.

'We'll go and visit them,' said Freddie, but Piotr said he didn't know where they were. 'We'll find them,' my brother insisted.

Piotr blinked away a tear and shook his head. He hated war, he said. It destroyed families.

Then we told him about Dad.

'They sent him to prison when he wouldn't kill anybody,' said Freddie. 'Then we had to go to Wales cos Mr and Mrs Bazley couldn't look after us.'

He asked if we had family in Wales but we said no.

'We miss Dad, don't we, Lizzie?'

When the bell rang for the end of visiting hour, Piotr grasped our hands in turn before we left.

'*Dziekuje*,' he said. 'Thank you.' Then he spoke to the man in the next bed who translated for us.

'Piotr says that he knows some important people and he will try to help you. It is not good for children to be without their family.'

Freddie looked at me and grinned. 'Lizzie,' he said. 'He's going to get Dad out of prison.'

Thirty-Five

Nothing much happened until Thursday afternoon, when Mr Jenkins from the town hall visited.

'Come in, Ivor,' said Uncle Ossie, and ushered him into the kitchen where Auntie Katie was sitting by the fire looking sad. We were all busy cleaning our shoes ready for school the next day.

Auntie Katie looked up without a smile or anything. 'Would you like a cup of tea?' she said.

But Mr Jenkins shook his head. 'No thank you, Katie. I've come with this letter,' he said, pulling a piece of paper out of his pocket. 'It came from London, see. Thought I ought to come round straight away. It's about the children.'

'What's that then?' asked Uncle Ossie.

'It seems that the top brass from the air force have been making a fuss about the children here.'

We stopped polishing our shoes and turned to listen. Freddie's eyes were wild with excitement.

'Fuss?' asked Uncle Ossie. 'What do you mean, fuss?'

'It seems they don't think it's right that these young-uns are kept from their family after all they did for that Polish pilot. Brave they were, saving him like that.'

Uncle Ossie looked baffled and he scratched his head. 'I know they were brave, Ivor Jenkins. But how can they live

194

with their father if he's in prison? Answer me that.'

We held our breath, waiting to hear when they were going to let Dad out of Wormwood Scrubs. *When? When? When?* That's what we wanted to know. I squeezed my eyes tight shut and held my breath, waiting for Mr Jenkins to speak.

'I know he's in prison, Ossie,' he said. 'But they've found there's an aunt up in Lancashire, see.'

An aunt? My spine turned to ice as I listened. I wanted to scream, *Not Aunt Dotty. Not her!* But I stood there, listening.

'That's the first we've heard about a relative, isn't it, Katie?' said Uncle Ossie, raising his eyebrows.

But Auntie Katie was in her own world, thinking about Gwilym and she didn't answer.

Mr Jenkins shifted nervously from one foot to the other. 'Well, it's like this, see. The aunt's making a fuss now.'

'More fuss?'

'Yes,' answered Mr Jenkins. 'The authorities have informed her that her brother is in prison and she wants to know where the children are.'

'Well, you know where they are. They're here with us and have been since before Christmas, man.'

'Thing is, Ossie, she wants to know why they weren't sent to her so she could look after them. She said it was her duty as a member of the family and what would people say if she abandoned her own niece and nephew. She was very cross, I believe.'

'Cross, is it? And what does she want to do about it?'

195

'She's coming down to fetch them as soon as she can get away.'

Uncle Ossie sighed. 'Well,' he said, 'I suppose it's only right that they should be with family. She is their aunt, after all.'

'She'll write to you and let you know when she's coming,' said Mr Jenkins. 'Then she'll take the children back to Rochdale.'

There was no holding Freddie. He leaped at Mr Jenkins, pounding his fists on the man's stomach and screaming, 'No! We won't go!' until Uncle Ossie pulled him away and wrapped his arms around him.

'There, there, Freddie,' he said. 'You like your auntie, don't you?'

'No, we don't,' said Freddie. 'She's horrible and bad-tempered, and she smacks us and she hates Dad because he won't kill Germans.'

'Is this true, Lizzie?'

I nodded.

'Well,' said Mr Jenkins, straightening his waistcoat, 'she's family, and it's only right you go and live with her. I don't think there's anything I can do about it.'

Days passed and, although we hadn't heard from Aunt Dotty, we were terrified that she would just turn up and take us back to Rochdale. But before that could happen, another letter came from Dad.

Dear Lizzie and Freddie,

By the time you read this I will be up in
Shropshire. I am going to work in a coal mine
because they are very short of men to dig
coal these days. They said I could either go
down the mine or stay in prison. Well, it seemed
that digging coal would be better than sitting
in this cold place sewing mail bags. At least
I will be helping to keep the fires burning
in people's houses. It makes me glad that I
will be keeping you warm in my own small
way.

Please send your letters to this address:
22 Prospect Terrace
Hadley
Shropshire

Your loving Dad

As soon as I read the letter, I knew what to do. 'Freddie,' I
said, 'we're going to Hadley to find Dad.'

Thirty-Six

That night, I told Joy our secret. She was my friend. She had been like a sister to me. 'I can't tell Auntie Katie and Uncle Ossie we're leaving because they'll stop us. And we can't go and live with Aunt Dotty. We just can't.'

Joy sat on the edge of my bed. 'I don't blame you. She sounds like a real witch. If I was in your shoes, I'd do the same. But I'll miss you.'

'You can come with us, Joy,' said Freddie, who had been fizzing with excitement ever since I'd told him the plan.

'Have you got enough money?' Joy asked. 'Train fares are expensive.'

'I think so,' I said, and we began to count all the money we had. We cut open the two small bags that were still in our coats where Peg and Kitty had sewn them at the farm and tipped the money onto the chest of drawers. Then there were the silver sixpences dear old Mr Bazely had pressed into our hands as we were sent off on the train to Wales. And last of all, there was the money Joy's family had given us at the Christmas party.

I counted it twice, just to make sure. 'We've got more than enough for our train fare,' I said.

Freddie started jumping around the room and bouncing up on the bed shouting, 'Hurray! Hurray! We're going to see Dad.'

When he had calmed down, we talked through the plan for the next morning. We had to look as though we were going to school as usual, even though it meant leaving some of our things behind. This was the plan:

Pack as much stuff as possible in my schoolbag.

Get dressed (two layers).

Have breakfast.

Leave at the usual time.

Walk Freddie to school as normal, but go past it.

Catch the bus to Llanelli.

Walk to the station and catch the train.

The plan was clear. 'I hope we can do this,' I said, biting my thumbnail.

'You're clever, Lizzie Butterworth,' said Joy. 'You'll do it all right. But I've got something for you.' Then she went across to her own bedroom and came back carrying a lipstick case. 'Take this,' she said. 'There's only a bit in it, but Cousin Enid gave it to me.'

'What do I want lipstick for?'

'Put it on at the station. It'll make you look older. You won't look like two kids running away then, will you?'

'Do you think so?'

'Oh yes. You'll look like a film star.'

We laughed and I gave Joy a hug which made me feel even worse about leaving her behind. I would really miss her.

Later, when it was time to go to bed, I wrote a note for Auntie Katie and Uncle Ossie.

I'm sorry we had to leave, but we hate Aunt Dotty and we won't go and live with her. We are going to find Dad in Shropshire. I'll write as soon as we get there so you won't worry about us.

Thank you for being kind.

Love from,
Lizzie and Freddie

I put it on the chest of drawers. Then, before I lay down to go to sleep, I went to the window for the last time. There were plenty of stars that night and Mum was right there in the middle of them all. 'By tomorrow night,' I told her, 'we'll be with Dad again.' And I knew she was pleased to hear it.

I lay on my bed going over the plan in my head, again and again. *Was there anything I had forgotten? Would everything go smoothly? Would we really find Dad in Hadley?* I don't remember falling asleep, but the next thing I heard was Uncle Ossie calling up the stairs and telling us it was time to get up.

Freddie and I leaped out of bed and put on the extra layers of clothes.

'Do we look all right?' I asked Joy when she came into our bedroom.

'You look as though you've been eating too much pudding,' she laughed. 'But no one will notice.'

We hurried downstairs and found Uncle Ossie stirring the porridge for breakfast. 'Doing anything nice at school today?'

he asked as he spooned the porridge into bowls and set them on the table in front of us.

'Not really,' said Joy. 'Spelling test. Boring maths. That's all. What are you doing, Daddy?'

'Oh, busy day,' he said. 'Got to get out before high water, see. There's a steamer coming in.'

We ate our porridge faster than usual, not daring to look at one another in case we gave anything away. Auntie Katie sat at the end of the table without speaking, her hands folded on her lap, her eyes staring blankly.

'Drink your tea, love,' Uncle Ossie said, pushing her cup towards her. But she shook her head, not once looking up at him. 'I keep telling you – it's no good worrying,' he said, gently putting his hand on her shoulder. 'Our Gwilym will be out there somewhere as sure as eggs is eggs. When they said he was lost, it only meant they don't know where he was, see.'

I knew Auntie Katie didn't believe him but she slowly lifted the cup and sipped the tea.

'That's my girl,' said Uncle Ossie, reaching for his coat off the hook. 'Why don't you go out and have a bit of fresh air, eh? We don't want you looking like an old washed-out rag when our Gwilym comes home, do we? He'll say, "Hey, Mammy. Where's those rosy cheeks of yours gone to?"'

Auntie Katie raised her head and as he kissed her on the cheek, she smiled. It was only a little smile but it was the first we had seen for days.

Once Uncle Ossie had left for work, she stood up, brushed

away the creases in her skirt and sighed with the effort of it. 'I think your Uncle Ossie's right,' she said quietly. 'Perhaps some fresh air will do me good.' Then she looked at us. 'You girls go and catch your bus and I'll take Freddie to school today.'

Thirty-Seven

Our plan was in ruins. If Auntie Katie took Freddie to school he couldn't get on the bus with us. She had never taken him before – except for his very first day. We always took him in the morning and she fetched him at home time. Every day.

When Auntie Katie's back was turned, I glanced across at Joy and she looked at me, her eyes wide with alarm. I lifted my hands, palms up, as if to say, *What do we do now?* and Joy shook her head meaning, *I don't know.* Freddie understood there was a problem and I reached out and squeezed his shoulder to remind him not to say a word.

We stood up, clearing the pots away and putting them in the sink as if nothing was wrong. I gritted my teeth, trying to make myself think. *Think! Think!*

It was then that Joy suddenly groaned. Quietly at first. Just one. Then more groans. Louder.

'What's the matter, Joy?' asked Auntie Katie. 'Are you all right?'

Joy turned to her mother, clutching her stomach. 'I think I'm going to…' before she could say another word, she ran out through the back door and down the path to the lavvy. She didn't come back for five minutes at least. When she did, she lurched forward into the kitchen, her face paper white.

'Feel bad, Mammy,' she said. 'Feel sick. Sorry.' She flopped onto a chair at the table and sank her head in her arms.

Auntie Katie leaned over her. 'You do look poorly,' she said, stroking her hair. 'Must be something you've eaten. I think you'd better stay home with me, eh?'

Slowly Joy raised her head and looked at her through half-closed eyes and nodded.

'Don't worry, Auntie Katie,' I said. 'I'll take Freddie to school. You stay and look after Joy. She looks really bad.'

We put on our coats and walked down the hall. As we shut the front door behind us, I felt like shouting, *Thank you, Joy! You're a genius!* She had even smothered her face with white-wash off the walls of the lavvy to make herself look pale. Double genius! She had given us the chance to get away.

Freddie and I hurried down the steps and set off along the road to catch the bus. I could hardly stop myself from running. I didn't even mind the cold wind blowing off the sea, bringing rain with it. We were on our way to Dad!

In five minutes, we were passing Freddie's school. Small children were heading towards the gate. Some with brothers and sisters. Others with mothers holding their hands.

'Look, Mammy, there's Freddie,' pointed one little girl. 'Where you going, Freddie?' she called. 'Is that your big sister?'

My heart began to race. This was one detail I hadn't thought about – meeting children who knew Freddie. 'Don't say a word,' I whispered as we hurried past. 'Pretend you didn't hear.'

'Freddie!' the girl shouted again. 'Aren't you coming?'

Her mother didn't even glance at us. 'Don't shout, Mavis,' she said, and she dragged the little girl towards the gate.

When we finally saw the bus stop ahead, there was a queue of people waiting to go to Llanelli. Some of them were girls from my school. 'Better hang back for a bit. I don't want any of them asking questions,' I told Freddie.

We waited in a shop doorway on the other side of the road until the bus came. Then we ran across, heads down, reaching it just as the last person was stepping on board.

That last person turned out to be Auntie Marged.

'Well, if it isn't Lizzie and Freddie,' she said as we climbed onto the bus. 'Where are you off to then?'

I didn't know what to say, but Freddie answered her brilliantly. 'Lizzie's taking me to the dentist. My tooth's been hurting all night.' And he put his hand to his cheek and rubbed it.

'Isn't your Auntie Katie taking you, little man?' she asked, settling into the seat in front of us.

Freddie shook his head, pulled his coat collar over his cheek and said nothing.

'She's looking after Joy,' I said. 'She's got terrible stomach ache. Something she's eaten, I think.'

Auntie Marged frowned and looked ever so worried. 'Oh dear,' she said. 'I should go with you myself and make sure that Freddie's all right. I'm sure Katie would want me to.'

My mouth went dry. 'Thanks ever so much,' I said, 'but he'll be OK. Honestly. And I know where the dentist is.'

'Well, as I say, I *should* go with you . . .'

'No, really—'

'But I can't, see. I've arranged to meet my cousin in Llanelli and she'll wonder where I am if I don't turn up. Normally, I'd help you out. Oh dear, I am sorry. Are you sure you'll be all right?'

I smiled in relief. 'Yes, thank you. I'll take care of Freddie.'

The bus soon reached Llanelli and we jumped off, anxious to get away from Auntie Marged. I hurried towards the station, tugging Freddie after me, wondering who else we were going to meet before we caught that train to Hadley.

Thirty-Eight

We were in the station before you could blink. I went into the ladies to put on the red lipstick Joy had given me, and when I came out, Freddie looked at me and pulled a face.

'What did you put that on for? It looks silly.'

'Joy said that the lipstick would make me look more like your grown-up sister, not a kid running away from school.'

She must have been right because when I went to the booking office, the man behind the glass said, 'Taking your little brother for a day out, are you?' and he gave me two tickets: one half-price, and one full fare.

We went and stood on the platform which was crowded with people waiting for the same train as us. I looked around, feeling nervous in case there was someone from Pwll. Joy's cousin, maybe, or her aunt or uncle – a neighbour, even. But I couldn't see anyone I recognised.

Freddie pushed his way to the front of the platform and bent forward, staring down the line, impatient for the train to arrive. 'I can't see it? When is it coming?'

'Just a few minutes, Freddie,' I said, pulling him back from the edge. 'It'll come soon and we'll be on our way.'

He didn't have to wait long. First came the announcement over the loud speakers. *'The train approaching platform two is the nine-ten for Shrewsbury.'* Seconds later, the black engine arrived, deafening us with its wheels grinding and grating on the tracks, and filling the station with smelly grey smoke. The brakes screeched as it came to a halt. Doors were flung open with bangs and clunks. People climbed out onto the platform, while those waiting to get on board pushed forward.

The crowd swept us along, and we held hands, afraid of losing each other, until someone lifted Freddie onto the train and I climbed up behind. Even the corridor, which ran the full length of the train, was crowded – but we managed to squeeze along until we found a carriage with one empty seat.

'You come in here, love,' said a large woman with a little girl on her knee. 'You can both fit in. Come on.'

A man sitting next to her put my bag and our gas masks onto the parcel shelf. Then we sat down as the guard blew the whistle. Doors banged shut, more whistle blowing and finally the train began to move. Freddie looked at me and grinned.

We were on our way!

There were four men in the carriage, all wearing RAF uniforms. They looked pale, and ever so tired. For most of the way they sat with their heads resting on the seat backs, and their eyes closed. I wanted to ask them if they knew Piotr but I didn't like to wake them. I bet they'd been out all night flying over Germany. They probably hated Adolf Hitler too.

It was a long, slow journey and the train seemed to stop at every station along the line. People got off and more got on. It was full all the way, and smelled of smoke and wet coats, and by the time we changed trains at Shrewsbury we were ravenous because we hadn't eaten since breakfast.

'I'm hungry, Lizzie,' Freddie wailed as we climbed into the new train. 'My tummy hurts.'

'Poor you,' said the lady opposite and she gave him a piece of bread out of her shopping basket and he was happy for a while.

When we finally arrived at Hadley station, I asked a porter where Prospect Terrace was.

'Go that way,' he said, pointing down the road. 'Past The Barley Mow and turn left. Are you visiting relatives, miss?'

'We're going to see our dad,' Freddie said. 'He works down a mine and gets coal for everybody.'

'Good man,' said the porter. 'But you'll have to hurry if you're going to get there before dark. You don't want your dad worrying, do you?'

As we headed for Prospect Terrace the light was fading. An icy wind made us feel hungrier than ever and when the smell of fish and chips drifted out of a small shop, we had to stop.

I pulled our last few coins out of my pocket. 'We've got enough for chips,' I said, and we went inside and stood in the queue until it was our turn.

'Just chips, please,' I said, and a parcel was passed to me over the counter. I felt heat coming through the newspaper wrapping, warming my hands.

As soon as we were out in the street, we opened the paper and steam rose off the chips. We crammed them into our mouths and felt them land warm and tasty into our empty stomachs.

'The best chips ever,' grinned Freddie, screwing up the paper and wiping his mouth on his sleeve.

We set off down the road and soon came to the corner and The Barley Mow pub.

'That's it.' I pointed up at the metal sign fixed on the wall. '*Prospect Terrace.* This is where Dad lives, Freddie.'

It was a long street of terraced houses, just like ours back home in Rochdale. There were numbers painted on the doors and Freddie ran ahead until he found number twenty-two in the middle of the row. Then he stood outside waiting for me to catch up. 'I'll knock,' he said, and thumped on the door, calling, 'Dad!' at the same time.

No one came. I bent down and shouted through the letter box too, just in case Dad was asleep upstairs. You never know. He might have been working shifts or something.

Dad didn't come, but the door of number twenty opened and a lady came out carrying a baby wrapped in a shawl. I expect she'd heard us shouting.

'Who are you looking for?' she said.

'Our dad,' Freddie told her. 'He lives here. We know he does.'

The lady shook her head. 'They're all up at the pit, ma duck,' she said. 'Because of the accident.'

I stared at her. 'But we've come to see our dad.'

Then the baby started to cry. 'It's cold out here,' she said. 'You'd best come in.' So we stepped into her living room. 'There's been an accident at the pit. Everybody's up there helping out. You're welcome to wait here, if you like.'

'But where's Dad? Do you live at number twenty-two as well?' Freddie asked.

The lady, who was called Mrs Thompson, laughed. 'No, duck. He lives next door with three other conchies. They're nice lads. Off to the pit every day, regular as clockwork.'

One question was on my mind. 'Did our dad go down the coal mine this morning?'

She stood there rocking the baby over her shoulder. 'Aye, all four of 'em went.'

My stomach knotted tight. I'd heard of pit accidents, and now our dad could be right in the middle of one.

'Don't you worry,' said Mrs Thompson, who could see we were panicked. 'The rescue team will be working night and day till they get 'em all out.'

Now Freddie understood that something was wrong. 'Is our dad stuck in a tunnel?'

Mrs Thompson sat on the settee and took hold of his hand. 'They'll go down and find him soon. I know they will. Don't you worry.'

But her words were drowned by Freddie, who made a terrible noise. 'I want my dad!' he yelled again and again.

Nothing would stop him, until Mrs Thompson promised to take us to the pit so we would be there when Dad came out.

Thirty-Nine

'I'll take the baby to number eighteen,' she said. 'Then we'll go and find your dad, eh?'

By the time we walked out of the house, it was dark. I looked up, hoping to see Mum's star, but the sky was cloudy and I couldn't see a single one. *How could she watch us? How could she take care of us?* I lagged behind Mrs Thompson and Freddie. 'If you're up there, Mum, please keep Dad safe,' I whispered, 'and bring him out of that mine. Those tunnels must be ever so dark.' There was just a chance she would hear me, and I knew she would do her best.

It was quite a walk up to the pit but when we got there people were standing around with lanterns and torches. Crowds of people. Just waiting. Not talking much.

'Any news?' Mrs Thompson asked a man who was holding a big book and a pencil.

'One dead,' he said, 'and three brought out injured, but not badly.' Then he looked over at us. 'Who are these two, Annie? This is no place for young-uns.'

'I had to bring 'em. They're after their dad, William Butterworth,' she said, craning her neck to peek at his book. 'Is he on your list?'

The man looked down at the page and shook his head. 'He's not out yet,' he said.

As he spoke, the pit wheel began to turn and the crowd rushed forward. We followed.

'What's happening?' I asked Mrs Thompson.

'The cage is coming up,' she said. 'Your dad might be in it.'

I could hardly stand still I was that bothered. My heart was pounding and Freddie obviously felt the same; he was jigging about, hopping from one foot to the other.

As the rusty old cage came into view I crossed my fingers and prayed Dad would be there.

The metal door clanged open, people surged in front of us towards the cage so that, even standing on tiptoe, I couldn't see much. Then the crowd parted to make way for the rescue team and I saw three stretchers. On each one there was a miner lying still, black with coal dust. As they were carried past the man with the book, the stretcher bearers called out names and he wrote them down.

'James Bradshaw,' said one. 'Injured.'

'Gwyn Davies,' called another. 'Injured.'

The third one shouted, 'Tom Millett,' and shook his head as he passed by. The miner's face was covered with a coat and I realised he must be dead. It was a terrible shock, but I stood in front of Freddie so he wouldn't see. At least it wasn't Dad.

Another lot of rescuers stepped into the cage and went down the mine while we waited again. The wind was bitter and getting colder all the time. Freddie was shivering, but no matter how Mrs Thompson tried she couldn't persuade him to leave and go back to her house.

213

By the time the rescuers came up again, it was late. We were frozen to the bone, blue with cold. But we wouldn't move. As the cage door opened, I hardly dared to look at the men who had come up and I felt a growing fear that Dad might never come out.

One by one, the injured were carried past the man with the book and into the ambulance. Names were called, but still William Butterworth was not one of them.

Mrs Thompson was explaining to Freddie that Dad was sure to be in the next cage, when I heard one of the rescuers call, 'There's been another rock fall and Will says he's not coming up till he's dug through to Fergus!'

I ran across and stood in front of him. 'Who's down there?' I said. 'Is William Butterworth?'

The man was black with grime and his face was running with sweat. 'William Butterworth?' he repeated, wiping his nose with a grimy handkerchief. 'Aye. That's him. He could have come up with us, but his pal's trapped behind a pile of rubble. Wall collapsed, see.'

I grabbed the man by his coat. 'They won't leave him will they, mister?' I asked as tears started to run down my cheeks. 'Say you promise! Will you tell him we're waiting for him and he has to come up?'

The man leaned forward and took hold of my hand. 'My name's Jimmie. Who are you, miss?'

'I'm Lizzie and my brother's Freddie and William Butterworth is our dad,' I said all in one breath.

Jimmie patted me on the shoulder. 'Don't you worry, lass.

They'll not leave him, and I'll make sure they tell him you're here. We'll get him out all right. Brave man, your dad.'

I knew Dad was still down there, hundreds of feet below the ground, but I felt really proud of him and, all of a sudden, I was sure he'd come out. He was staying down there to rescue his friend. Our dad was a hero.

Mrs Thompson finally persuaded us to go inside a little shed not far away, and somebody brought some soup. When we'd finished drinking it, she took Freddie on her knee. I sat next to her and she wrapped her arm round my shoulders.

'They'll be a while before they come up again,' she said, 'so why don't you close your eyes for a bit?'

I leaned against her, aching with tiredness and worry and, although I tried to stay awake, I couldn't. I dropped into a sleep as deep as the ocean until I felt Mrs Thompson shaking me awake. 'Lizzie,' she whispered. 'Come on. Jimmie thinks they've brought your dad up.'

I sat bolt upright, thinking it was a dream at first. But she said it again. 'Jimmie's just told me,' she said. And I believed her.

I leaped to my feet and ran through the door, leaving Freddie still asleep on her lap. I pushed through the grown-ups until I bumped into Jimmie.

'Steady on, lass,' he said, grabbing hold of my arm. 'Let the stretchers come through. You'll see soon enough.'

The first stretcher reached the man with the book. 'Fergus O'Donell. Injured,' called his rescuer. And the man wrote it down.

That was the name of Dad's friend. I was sure of it. His clothes were torn and bloody and his face was twisted with pain. I hoped Dad wouldn't be injured too. *Please let him be all right,* I said to myself. *Please. Please.*

Then came the second stretcher. This time the man was covered with a grey blanket.

'Edward Johnson,' the stretcher bearer said, and he shook his head.

Jimmie gripped my shoulder as the last stretcher was carried slowly by. I couldn't see the man's face clearly and even when I squeezed my eyes, I couldn't tell if it was Dad. But it had to be. I willed it to be Dad. It was the last stretcher.

I wrenched myself free from Jimmie's grip and pushed someone out of the way to get nearer. But even when I was close up, all I could see was the thick black coal dust coating the man's face and I still couldn't tell if it was Dad.

My stomach sank as I watched the rescuers take him to the man with the book.

Then one called out, 'William Butterworth. Injured.'

Forty

Dad was taken to the hospital but we weren't allowed to visit him cos they said we were too young. We were hopping mad and Freddie cried a lot, so in the end Mrs Thompson took us up there anyway and made a terrible fuss on our behalf.

'It's not right!' she said to the matron, who was twice as big as she was and had a long droopy nose and a mouth that turned down at the edges. 'You shouldn't stop them visiting their father. He's been in here for two days and his kids still haven't seen him.'

The matron stood with her arms crossed, blocking our way. 'There are rules in my hospital,' she said in a snooty voice. 'Hospital wards are not suitable for children. They can't go in.'

Mrs Thompson wasn't a bit scared of her. 'Is that so?' she said, raising her umbrella and shaking it at her. 'If you think I'll let a bossy woman like you stop us, you can think again.' And I swear she was going to hit her.

The matron's frilly cap quivered on her head. Whether it was from temper or fear, I don't know.

'It's been long enough,' insisted Mrs Thompson, and she pushed past her, dragging us through the double doors. I think the matron was shocked. She didn't follow us.

When we found Dad's ward, we spotted him straight away and raced down to his bed and nearly hugged him to death.

'Watch it, you two,' he said. 'I'm a bit sore.' But he was grinning and I knew he was as glad to see us as we were to see him.

His arm was in a sling and there was a big bump at the bottom of the bed.

'What's that?' I asked.

'It's a cage,' he explained. 'It's to stop children like you jumping on my legs.'

'What's wrong with your legs?' asked Freddie.

Dad reached out and held his hand. 'Nothing much, little man.' But he changed the subject after that. I don't think he wanted to talk about it.

He looked up at Mrs Thompson and smiled. 'I hear you've been looking after my terrible two,' he said. 'I'm very grateful, thank you. I know they're a real handful.'

Mrs Thompson laughed. 'Think nought about it, lad. They're a grand pair. But I didn't contact the authorities or anybody. I thought I'd better speak to you first.'

'Aunt Dotty was coming to get us,' Freddie interrupted. 'So we had to run away. You wouldn't want us to go and live with her, would you, Dad?'

He smiled. 'I suppose not but you must both promise that you'll write at once to Aunt Dotty and explain that you're here with me. And say thank you for offering to look after you both.'

We nodded, but Freddie pulled a face.

'And I want you to write to Mrs Roberts.'

'I left her a note, Dad.'

'Write and tell her you're safe, Lizzie. She'll be worried. And write to Arthur and Lalia, too.'

'It'll take ages,' said Freddie. 'Do we have to?'

Dad nodded. 'Indeed you do, because I can't,' he said, lifting his injured arm. So I had to agree.

I wrote the letters like I promised. Freddie tried to help but his spelling wasn't very good and it took him ages to write anything so he drew some pictures instead.

We stayed with Mrs Thompson and visited Dad every day and that matron never said a word to us again. I don't think she wanted to have another argument with Mrs Thompson.

Then one morning there was a knock at the front door. When I opened it I had the biggest shock ever. There on the pavement were Arthur and Lalia! For a second I just stared, my mouth open like a fish. I couldn't speak.

'Can we come in, then?' said Arthur, standing there with his big bushy beard and twinkling eyes.

When my voice came back it was a high-pitched squeal, and I flung my arms around them both. 'I can't believe it's you!' I said. 'I can't believe it!'

'Who is it, Lizzie?' called Freddie, who was crayoning at the table. And when Arthur and Lalia stepped inside and he saw them, he leaped off his chair and threw himself at Arthur, clinging to his legs before flinging himself at Lalia and hugging her too. 'Where's Jip?' he asked. 'Where's Bernardo and Basil? Why haven't they come with you? Where are they?'

Lalia laughed. 'Slow down, Freddie. We'll tell you our news all in good time.'

Mrs Thompson was in the back yard hanging out the washing but when she heard the commotion she came rushing in to see Arthur and Lalia standing in the living room.

'These are our friends,' Freddie explained. He could hardly stand still he was that excited. 'They've come to see us.'

Mrs Thompson wiped her hands on her pinny. 'Oh, I'm really glad you're here,' she said with a smile as wide as Blackpool beach. 'They've told me all about you. Come in and sit down.'

And she went and put the kettle on.

I suppose you're wondering what happened after that. Well, we had a big discussion with Dad. He wanted us to go back to Whiteway with Arthur and Lalia, but we couldn't leave him in that hospital with that horrible matron and nobody to come and talk to him and make him laugh. Could we?

'We're not going,' we told him. 'We're staying here.'

Mrs Thompson was ever so kind and let us live with her until Dad was well again and out of hospital. Then Basil came to fetch us and took us all back to Whiteway. And that's where we are now, living with Arthur just like we used to.

We're all saving up to pay back the money Kitty and Peg gave us. Dad says we must. We wrote and told them everything that had happened after we left the farm and we had a lovely letter back from them.

Joy sent us a letter, too. And there was good news. It turned out that Gwilym hadn't been killed after all. He'd been taken prisoner by the Germans. They'd even had a letter from him and that made Auntie Katie and Uncle Ossie really happy. When the war's over, he'll come home, Joy said.

Dad's not as strong as he was, and his chest gives him a lot of trouble, but we look after him and take Jip on walks and have fun together. Dad's learning to walk again – Lalia helps him a lot and he's getting better all the time. He says that one day soon he'll be able to race Basil down the path. I bet our dad will win.

Things are a lot easier now we don't have to hide. The police aren't interested in Dad any more. He couldn't be a soldier with his legs the way they are. On days when he's feeling well enough, he goes over to the workshop and does small repair jobs. But he says that he'll soon be back to normal and then he'll be able to fix cars and machinery and stuff. He's good at that.

Freddie and I go to the school in Miserden with Bernardo, which is not too bad – although every now and then the evacuees call us names. But who cares? That's what I say.

We're all together and our life at Whiteway is happy.

When I lie in bed at night, I sometimes wonder about the war and who is brave and who is a coward. I think that you have to be brave to stand up for what you believe in. It's not only soldiers who are the brave ones. The people they leave behind have to be brave too, living with rationing and air raids and being separated from their families.

That's what Mum thinks too. She told me.

Acknowledgements

With thanks to Charlie Sheppard my wonderful editor whose suggestions were invaluable and to my agent, Annette Green, for her support and enthusiasm. To all those people who gave their time to tell me stories of their lives in 1942. Joy Thacker whose knowledge of the history of Whiteway was so helpful and Yolande Creed who made me welcome in her home and walked me around the Whiteway colony. To Joy Clayton-Jones whose memories of a Welsh childhood were vivid and invaluable. To John Powell for information about trains. To Anita Davies, Katie Forster, Marion Jones and Dave Margaroni for their help and enthusiasm.

Notes from the author

Although I invented the characters in *Run Rabbit Run*, the story is based on true events. The places in the book are all real. For example, Whiteway still exists. The Colony Hall is still there and used for meetings once a month. Protheroe's Bakery is there, too, but is now closed. As for the railway carriages where Basil lived, they were taken away shortly after the end of the war. The community at Whiteway consists of artists, craftspeople, a masseur and a blacksmith. The paths leading to houses are still unmade and hardly the width of a car.

In the Second World War there were over sixty thousand conscientious objectors like William Butterworth. When they went before a tribunal like William did, they were rarely given full exemption from fighting unless they had careers in social work or church projects or medicine. Many conscientious objectors worked as stretcher bearers on the battlefield, which was incredibly dangerous. But others refused to play any part in a process that led to killing. Like William, many were sent to prison.

DANGEROUS DIAMONDS

BARBARA MITCHELHILL

When Dad goes missing, twins Harry and Charlie
scour Edinburgh to find him. But why are others
determined to stop them? And how is a strange
wooden box linked to his disappearance? The
twins soon find they are in terrible danger but
push themselves to the limit in their attempt to
outwit those who are holding
their father.

'An adventure thriller full of
strong characters and deceit, this
book enthrals the reader from
the very beginning.'
School Librarian

9781842709788 £4.99

STORM RUNNERS

BARBARA MITCHELHILL

When dramatic storms batter a small Scottish island and reduce a village to ruins, Ally and Kirstie think that they are the only survivors. But then they meet Brad, the son of American scientists, and together they uncover the terrifying truth about the storms and the man who controls them.

'The tension and excitement never let up from the first page to the last in this immensely readable and thrilling adventure story.'
Northern Echo

9781842706404 £4.99

When You Reach Me

REBECCA STEAD

Miranda's life is starting to unravel. Her best friend, Sal, gets punched by a kid on the street for what seems like no reason, and he shuts Miranda out of his life. Then the key Miranda's mum keeps hidden for emergencies is stolen, and a mysterious note arrives:

'I am coming to save your friend's life, and my own. I ask two favours. First, you must write me a letter.'

The notes keep coming, and whoever is leaving them knows things no one should know. Each message brings her closer to believing that only she can prevent a tragic death. Until the final note makes her think she's too late.

Winner of the John Newbery Medal 2010

Winner of the *New York Times Notable Book* and *Publishers' Weekly Best Children's Book*

'Smart and mesmerising'
New York Times

9781849392129 £5.99

The Unfinished Angel

SHARON CREECH

'Peoples are strange!
The things they are doing and saying — sometimes they make
no sense. Did their brains fall out of their heads?'

Angel is having an identity crisis when he meets Zola —
a talkative young girl who moves into Angel's tower
high in the Swiss Alps. 'This Zola is a lot bossy,' Angel
thinks. But out of their bickering an unexpected
friendship forms, and their teamwork is about to benefit
the entire village . . .

Sharon Creech won the Carnegie Medal and the
Newbery Medal, and was shortlisted
for the Costa Award. She has sold
over one million copies of her
books worldwide.

'Inventive, sassy and gutsy . . . *The
Unfinished Angel* . . . is an endlessly
witty and life-affirming read.'
Booksellers' Choice,
The Bookseller

9781849390835 £5.99

Holly

STARCROSS

BERLIE DOHERTY

'Do you know who I am?'

Holly has never really thought about it. But then her internet friend Zed asks her name, and a mysteriously familiar man starts driving around and asking after her. She is going to have to explore the long-forgotten life her mother ran away from eight years before, and find out who she really is.

'A beautiful, moving story with characters to believe in and a sense of the uniqueness of every human life.' TES

BERLIE DOHERTY is twice winner of the Carnegie Medal.

9781842709306   £5.99

Follyfoot

MONICA DICKENS

Follyfoot farm is a home for rescued and unwanted horses, and the animals are cared for by the stable-hands Callie, Dora and Steve. There's plenty of work to be done around the farm, but there's still always time for the mysteries and adventures that happen at Follyfoot.

Visitors are welcome at the farm, but when two boys come snooping round and obviously aren't interested in the horses, Callie is suspicious. She's sure she recognises one of them. But where from? The mystery deepens and it's up to the young stable-hands to get to the bottom of it.

A long-awaited reissue of the novel that inspired a generation of horse-lovers!

www.follyfootbooks.co.uk

9781849391306 £4.99